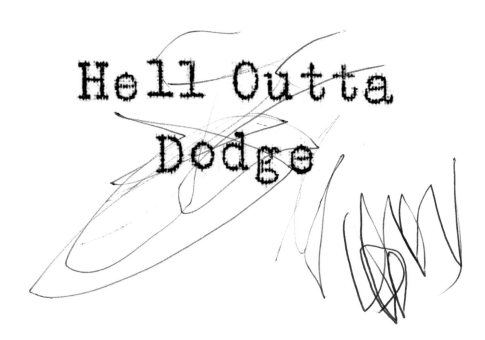

Hell Outta Dodge

Fay Campbell
Nancy Orum

Dedicated to our big brothers,
Paul and Wade,
and our children, who are finally
old enough to read this.

Don't poke no beans up your nose.

CAMPIAN BELLSTONE PUBLISHERS
Richmond, Virginia, USA
www.BellstoneBooks.com

Hell Outta Dodge
by Fay Campbell & Nancy Orum
Edited and designed by Ian F. Wesley
ISBN 978-1-940670-00-3

1. Fiction   2. Drama
3. Supernatural   4. Friendship
5. Coming-of-Age

Cover Photo by Mat Hayward

This book is available in
paperback and e-book editions

Table of Contents

Acknowledgments

by Fay Campbell

Writing with my sister, Wonder Woman, my hero, was one of the coolest things I've ever done.

Thanks, Ian, for delivering this baby.

by Nancy Orum

I have had the time of my life writing this book with my sister, Fay. She is without a doubt the smartest, wittiest person I know. Put us together for five minutes and we laugh so hard we might just wet our pants.

Chip, the boy down the block, you've been by my side for 40-plus years. You are my rock and inspiration. I loved you then, and I love you now. Thanks for all you do. It's a lot!

Donell, you are never far from my thoughts.

Mom, you are my role model and my friend.

Nick, Jess, Greg and J.J., you are the best part of my life.

Solomon, Poppy and Townsend, you are my heart.

Ian, thanks for believing in us.

Prologue

Once, when summers lasted forever, there was always time to spread blankets on the grass and watch the clouds change shapes in endless parades. We powdered our noses yellow with dandelions, wore purple violets in our hair, and sucked the sweetness from pink clover. We were on a first name basis with the trees in the neighborhood, and in their leafy security the only evil we had to fear was monsters under the bed.

We quenched our thirst with lemonade, ate cookies, and ate fruit fresh from the trees. We knew so many things, and there was always a right answer. We pretended away any problems we had. Sometimes, we had to pretend so hard that the boundaries between fantasy and reality melted.

As long as we held on tight, the trees and our friendship made us strong. We had everything we needed. Together we were willows that bent in the face of high winds and remained strong.

Witchy Woman

THE EAGLES

Echoed voices in the night,
She's a restless spirit
on an endless flight.

Kailin Center always gave Justice the creeps. The long, narrow hallways were recently painted an institutional green, but were insidiously turning drab and colorless. The walls seemed to suck the color out of the paint the way Kailin Center itself seemed to suck the life out of its residents. Nevertheless, he came to visit and talk with his catatonic mother no less than once a month. The nurses and doctors at the psychiatric facility assured him that he need not disrupt his life because in her vegetative state she didn't even realize he was there. They didn't understand.

"Soon, Mother, soon it will be all taken care of," he said without taking his clear, gray eyes off the pale woman. "Then I can let you go." Justice reflected on the work he had accomplished in the past couple of years. "Just one more thing—one more—and then I can get on with my life."

He was sixteen when his mother's condition worsened to the point where he could no longer care for her alone. She taught him to rely on himself when he was just a child. So when he graduated from high school early, he was more than prepared to live on his own. But, by then his mother needed constant care.

It was just after he placed her in Kailin Center that he found her old diary, and he became driven to avenge her. The origin of his name was crystal clear to him then. It was a message that his mother had sent to him through the wall surrounding her soul. His single-mindedness was about to pay off.

Although it had been a lifetime away, Justice could remember the times when his mother and he had a normal life. He could remember her taking him to ride a carousel on Saturday mornings, although he was too young to remember where the carousel was. He remembered eating pancakes on Sunday mornings. She always let him smother them with syrup. He didn't realize until she started to fail that they were quite poor. He never felt poor with her around.

He looked at the shriveled form centered on the hospital bed in front of him. In this small, frail person was the whole of his existence—his history, purpose and soul were contained inside this woman. He thought about his mission, how it was right, just and perfect. He had been the center of her universe while he was growing up, and now fate had obliged him to live for her, but time was running out. He had an urgent need to fulfill his quest. It must be finished before this tiny package in front of him totally disappeared.

Take Me Home, Country Roads

JOHN DENVER

Drivin' down the road,
I get a feelin' that I should have
been home yesterday.

Sigley, population 347, was the last little town on her route home. It looked the same as it did twenty years ago. It was a gritty little town nestled in the crook of the river. In the winter, bald eagles nested there. In the summer, the river bugs got so thick there were times you dare not open your mouth outside. For the past ten miles Jayne had been preparing herself for the sight of Sigley and the memories it would bring back. As she always did when she drove through, she considered driving by Peter's parents' house. Although she never actually took that detour, the thought always shamed her. She wondered if other thirty-eight year-old psychotherapists felt like a truck had driven over them when they thought about their high school sweethearts.

As she passed by her personal landmarks in the village—the little park where they played horse and rider, the tiny grocery store where they bought fudge

bars and Green Rivers—bittersweet memories flooded
Jayne's mind. She remembered how she fell into the
blueness of Peter's eyes and his salty-sweet smell. And
she remembered the pain of losing him.

It was a sort of sadness she felt—a gnawing feeling,
just below her stomach. Since that hellish incident at
work two years ago, Jayne had become quite used to
that feeling. She reminded herself that this was going
to be a few days away from her career. This was a time
to help a friend, not a time to mourn the loss of her
practice and her perfect world.

The only stop sign in town was next to the front
yard of a house that was pure Sigley. It was a little
yellow house with a green roof and a slightly crooked
porch that wrapped around two sides. In a blue plastic
wading pool just off the porch, sat two little girls. A
third girl was pouring water out of a Tupperware bowl
over her squealing friends. The girls looked to be about
four years old and wore crayon-colored swimsuits that
tied behind their necks. A woman stood guard. Jayne
knew she was a full-time mother because, after all,
this was Sigley. Of course there was no traffic, so Jayne
lingered at the stop sign and watched with a combina-
tion of delight and sadness, until she realized that the
mother was nervously staring at her.

Until two years ago, Jayne didn't know how it felt to
be perceived as a threat. She didn't like the feeling. For
a split second she felt the urge to quell the fears of the
young mother.

"Jayne Lipton, a threat in Sigley?" She spoke the words and smiled ever so slightly as she left the stop sign.

The fifteen-minute drive from Sigley to her hometown of Dodge spanned several years of memories. The narrow highway still had grass growing between its two lanes. The "hard road" they call it here. She laughed, "Hard road." It certainly was a hard road—a difficult one to travel. From its surface, unbidden childhood memories pushed their way into her thoughts and took over for the rest of the drive.

She remembered when she got her first pair of glasses. She was two. That day, her father carried her from the car to the house and set her down inside the front door like a parcel. Her parents were talking quietly and she knew it was about her, but she was too awestruck to listen. She was busy discovering her house. The floors were made of individual strips and were not just solid brown. The bright pink and green blobs on the walls in the bathroom were graceful, long-necked birds under palm trees—each standing on only one of her long legs.

When she was much older, her mother told her that she couldn't possibly have remembered those events, because she was so young. But, you don't forget the first time you see things as they really are.

It couldn't have been too long after that when she first met Mebo. Mary Elizabeth Briget O'Cullin. The two of them grew up across the street from each other.

Mebo had lots of brothers and sisters, so their house was always noisy and full of activity, very different from Jayne's. Mebo's parents had drinks together when her father came home from the bank. Jayne's parents were older and more sedate, and her household was much quieter and settled.

When they were in junior high school, Jayne thought Mebo's family was about the best family a kid could have. From across the street, everyone looked happy and successful and popular. Mebo always knew how to have a good time, and her right-and-wrong-o-meter didn't interfere with her social life the way Jayne's did. It didn't seem to matter to Mebo that she made fun of kids who were poor or different; she was always polite to their faces.

Jayne, on the other hand, had a real problem with guilt. She often wished she was more like Mebo, so she could join the *in* group in their laughter about scum, retards and cootie people. But, she always felt driven to go out of her way to be nice to the twin sisters who were both in special education class and together weighed a ton. She felt obligated to be nice to the skinny boy in her class who tried never to talk, because he stuttered so badly he could never finish whatever it was he had to say. The teachers left him pretty much alone, and Jayne was unsure whether they were sparing him from humiliation or if they were just too impatient to hear him out.

On holidays, especially Christmas, the difference

between the two families was particularly noticeable to Jayne. Mebo's family always had perfectly-flocked trees with twinkle lights and matching ornaments. Jayne wanted a tree like that so badly that she cried in her bedroom after she and her parents decorated theirs with ornaments collected over the years. And, in the twinkle of a light, she felt the guilt associated with wanting more than she had. She felt compelled to hang the ugly, broken angels on prominent branches because they reminded her of those people everyone laughed at, and she wanted them to feel cherished. She was careful not to let her parents see her cry about the tree. Even then she was a bit neurotic.

Jayne figured Mebo was normal and she was envious of that. Mebo concentrated on doing instead of feeling. Jayne didn't believe her friend was very much aware of her own feelings, let alone anyone else's—a bit shallow maybe, but not cruel.

Then there was Annie. Jayne remembered the first time they met. Well, the first time she heard about her anyway. Jayne and Mebo were playing cowgirl on the fence around Mebo's back yard, discussing the impending start of second grade. They had been assigned the same teacher and had already bought their school supplies. Mebo got a box of 64 Crayolas, but Jayne couldn't justify asking her mother for more than the required box of eight. Mebo kept talking about the new girl, Annie.

Mebo talked about this new girl too much and with

too much enthusiasm. Jayne took immediate action and persuaded her friend to take a solemn oath. They stood on opposite sides of the gate, clasped hands, and swore that they would be best friends forever. They vowed that anything that was Mebo's was half Jayne's and anything that was Jayne's was half Mebo's. The contract seemed to have included Annie.

Annie's family had just moved to town. Her father worked at the new power plant on the river that had brought so many other families to the area. Annie and her brother knew so much more about the world than Jayne and Mebo did, probably because they had lived somewhere besides Dodge. Annie told the girls stories of the town where she had lived in Iowa that had two swimming pools and a miniature golf course. Mebo and Jayne thought that was the height of sophistication. Annie's family rented a small house in Jayne's neighborhood that summer and later bought a big house on the top of the hill.

The day before the three of them began second grade, Jayne and Mebo went to Annie's house to play in her back yard. They played army with Annie's brother's new air guns that made loud, realistic noises when they were fired. Bud and Jayne tried to capture Annie and Mebo.

Mebo had just been marched to the prison under the clothesline when Annie's mother came outside carrying a large laundry basket full of sheets to hang on the line. She looked fearful. Jayne yelled out hello to her and waved. Mrs. McDonald glanced up and weakly smiled back. Even when she smiled, the worried expression never left her face. She looked over her shoulder to the back door.

The game stopped abruptly when Annie's dad stormed out of the house. He staggered toward his wife with a beer bottle in his hand, screaming filthy words at her—words Jayne and Mebo had never heard a dad use before. He pushed Annie's mother and she fell back through the hanging sheets. Jayne's reaction was to run over to help Mrs. McDonald, but Annie grabbed her arm and urgently pleaded that they go back to Jayne's house.

They quickly walked the block and a half without getting permission from anyone. On the way there, Annie acted as though nothing unusual had happened. Jayne and Mebo, however, were frantic. When Jayne wanted to run to her house to call the police or an ambulance, Annie looked at them with tears pooled in her eyes and whispered, "No, you don't understand! That would only make things *worse*. She's okay, she always is." That was the end of that. The three never discussed it again.

As they grew up, Jayne realized that Annie wanted Mebo's life even more than Jayne did. Whenever Annie was around Mebo's big, noisy, happy family, her eyes filled with longing. Annie drank in Mebo's family, trying to absorb every laugh and every kind word.

It was difficult for Jayne to remember the days before Annie joined her and Mebo and balanced them out, creating The Three. Jayne wondered if God purposely placed them all together in the world of Dodge. They shared each other's lives, each taking from the others what was missing in her own. Thirty years later, The Three were still sharing more than they knew.

Jayne felt the hard road loosen its grip a bit as the car sneaked into Dodge. She tried not to destroy the picture in her mind of The Three.

You always did see things the way you wanted to see them, Jayne. My memories are a bit different.

Jayne sighed in reply. The purpose of this trip was to help Annie get through her dad's funeral. She didn't have time or energy to deal with ghosts now.

Bad Moon Rising

CREDENCE CLEARWATER REVIVAL

I fear rivers overflowing.
I hear the voice of rage and ruin.

"Crap, what am I doing? I swore I'd never go back to that one-horse, piss-ant town, and here I am on a Friday morning, stuck on a fourteen-seat puddle-jumper on my way to Peoria so I can rent a Dodge and drive to Dodge."

Annie screamed inside her head again. She stared out the window and her jaw ached from clenching her teeth tightly enough to keep the screaming in.

"I need to remember to tell my shrink about the way I scream inside my head," she muttered to herself. "I might as well admit right now that eleven years of grief and therapy are down the fucking tubes."

Annie wondered what rock the other passengers had crawled out from under and what sins she had committed to be sharing a plane with a family of nine sticky, grimy, obnoxious kids and parents she swore were first cousins. Kids drove her crazy. At least that was one good thing to come out of the hysterectomy she had a year ago. She liked the idea that she could have lots of sex and get no kids, while Mebo had lots of kids and probably got no sex.

"I can't blame Mebo on that count," Annie thought. "I wouldn't go to bed with that redneck husband of hers on a bet. Well, not anymore. Maybe she came to her senses after five kids. As Mebo would no doubt say, 'Who'd a thunk it?'"

She realized how badly she needed a drink and found herself grasping a bottle of Valium in her purse. She needed to prepare for the inevitable voice.

So you've really got it bad, huh, Annie?

"Leave me alone, Sarah!" hissed Annie at her own reflection in the window. "What can I do about it now, anyway? Am I supposed to be miserable for the rest of my life? Am I supposed to stay away from The Three because you didn't know how to keep your pants on? What do you want? Did you want me to tell your parents about you and Bob? Is that it? Just fucking leave me alone! How can you continue to come between me and the rest of The Three? Why don't you just stay dead?"

Annie glanced around the plane to see if anyone was eavesdropping on her conversation with herself, but then she realized that the people on the plane wouldn't recognize a little insanity as anything unusual. Annie was heartily sorry that they didn't serve drinks on puddle-jumpers. She really needed one. Her ears popped as the plane began its descent.

"This weekend is going to be hell by numbers. I hope I can get a good martini in Dodge." She looked up to see the mother of the sticky tribe studying her with a tooth-deficient grin and realized that she was still talking out loud.

As much as she hated him, Annie wasn't looking forward to burying her father. The plane landed with a series of bumps and hops. Even the little plane was unsure if it wanted to be there. She felt a shiver of relief and dread when she climbed off the plane—the first step through the looking glass.

It wasn't hard to find her luggage, since her suitcases were the only parcels on the belt that didn't have A&P written on their sides. She stopped at the car rental counter to pick up the keys to the Dynasty.

She wished they still made Darts. It would be fitting to drive home in a Dodge Dart. The Dodge Darts were undefeated her senior year. That made her smile. For the rest of the drive home she dug deep for pleasant memories—Mebo leading cheers, long, pink prom dresses, and the sweet protection of Happy Mountain. There was a lot she couldn't remember, a lot she wouldn't remember, and the rest were memories of Dodge and The Three.

Help!

THE BEATLES

When I was younger,
so much younger than today,
I never needed anybody's
help in any way.

"Bob, how long are you going to be out?" called Mebo.

Bob yelled back over his shoulder, "Hell, Briget, you ought to know by now ..." His voice was lost in the normal clamor of the house as he slammed the door behind him.

To Annie and Jayne, she had always been Mebo, but Bob insisted that she go by her third name, Briget. It was his way of separating her from The Three and connecting her more securely to him. Annie knew that.

"Why does everybody try to separate The Three?" Mebo muttered.

Belinda screamed from her crib, tearing Mebo back to the present. Benny yelled at the baby to shut up. Then Brad turned up the volume of the cartoons loud enough to drown out the roar from Bob's tractor.

Mebo wished she hadn't let the twins sleep over at their friend's last night. She wished they'd stayed home to help her with the kids and the house. She wished it hadn't rained last night on the load of diapers she left on the clothesline. She wished things were different. She stood staring at the chaos as if she were seeing it for the first time.

She shook the wishes from her head and made her way through the piles of toys and laundry to get Belinda from her crib. The baby stopped crying and smeared teething biscuit kisses on her mom's face. Mebo threw a pile of towels off the rocking chair and sat down with the baby. "Oh, Beebee, what are Annie and Jayne going to think of this house? What are they going to think about you?"

Belinda squealed at her mother in delight and patted her face with sticky, dimpled hands.

Mebo instinctively rocked and patted the baby, but her mind was elsewhere. "I wonder what Annie will be wearing?" She turned her face toward her baby and continued, "When we were in the fourth grade, Annie used to copy the way I looked. She bought dresses that were just like mine. She was even jealous of me, Beeb, when I made cheerleading in high school, not to mention that I was dating the most popular guy in school. All she ever talked about was getting married and having kids."

She glanced over at the two pictures of Bob and her that sat among the kids' school pictures on the piano. Both were taken in their senior year of high school. One was the night of prom, when Mebo's long thick red hair fell in soft curls past her shoulders. "What made me think that pink was my color?" At the time she really loved that dress, daisies and all. Bob was so handsome in his rented tux—dark, black hair and those incredible gray eyes. The other picture of them was taken in their uniforms—the captain of the Dodge Dart football team and the captain of the cheerleading squad. "Glory days," Mebo thought. It never occurred to her that there were no current pictures of Mr. and Mrs. Bob Dorman.

"Deep down I think Annie always thought she'd end up with your daddy."

The baby studied a loose button on Mebo's shirt.

"And then after Annie went away to college, she never looked back. Now she's some big deal publisher in New York, when *I'm* the one who always did her English term papers."

The screen door slammed behind the twins and brought Mebo back.

"It's about time you two got home. I really need some help around here. You know Annie and Jayne will be here soon and I don't want them to think we live like this."

"But this *is* the way we live, Mom," Bella and Betsy said in unison.

Mebo hated it when they talked together. It made her think there was a conspiracy or at least a joke. "But they can't *know* this is the way we live."

"Why do you really care about these people or what

they think, anyway?" Betsy asked, "You call them your best friends, so how come we never see them?"

"Yeah, Mom, get a life," Bella mumbled under her breath.

"This is my life, Bella, the only one I have," she was very close to crying now. "It's just that things change. When I was your age I thought I knew how life would be, but it … it didn't work out right." Mebo withdrew again. "I missed something."

We all made big mistakes, didn't we, Mebo?

"Please go away, Sarah. I don't have time to sit and cry today," she mumbled to herself still rocking. "How do you always know when they're coming?"

The girls stared at her. They looked a little worried and when she looked back at them, a little annoyed. They glanced at each other, and Bella said to her mother, "I'll try to figure out the laundry if Betsy tries to find the floor."

Going Out of My Head

LITTLE ANTHONY AND THE IMPERIALS

And I think I'm going out of my head,
'Cause I can't explain the tears that I shed
over you.

The Dynasty crept into the driveway. Annie looked up at the house and noticed the new putty-colored siding. She turned off the ignition and was assaulted by unwelcome memories.

The last time she sat in this driveway was a year and a half ago, after her father picked her up from the airport in his beloved pickup truck. Ruby, he called it. She kept talking then, non-stop, in an attempt to maintain some control over the conversation. Remembering the last time she saw her father, she could almost smell his cigar breath. She could almost hear the drunken curses he flung at her as she left the house last Christmas. The memory of her own words echoed in her ears, "I will never come to this place again as long as *you* live!"

"Annie. *Annie.*" Aunt Pattie's voice and her tapping on the window tore Annie away from the memories.

"Annie, Hon, are you all right?" Patti didn't wait for an answer. "Come on in here, now, Hon. Your mother needs you to be strong for her, Sweetie."

It was difficult for Annie to climb out of the big car with her Aunt Patti pulling on her arm.

"Slow down, Salmon Patti," Annie winked at her aunt. The childhood name made the old woman stop pulling on Annie's arm for a second and smile at her niece. Patti quickly returned to the task at hand.

"Your mother is taking this really hard, Hon," Patti clucked the words and sounded like a corporal briefing her C.O. "Of course, it's only natural for her to be upset, but I don't know ... she hasn't even cried yet." Patti's hold on Annie's arm tightened as they walked up to the back door of the house. She whispered all this information into Annie's ear.

Patti was in her element. She was Annie's father's only sister. She never married, and so she tried to keep very close tabs on everyone else's families. But for all her love of gossip, Patti didn't know the big secrets.

As Annie was led into the house she felt herself stiffen and tasted something sour in the back of her throat. "I've got to hold on," Annie thought. "This is not a place where it's safe to show any weakness."

She surveyed the kitchen and steadied herself by touching the gold-flecked Formica countertop. Everything was in perfect order. On the counter two apple pies were cooling on trivets in the shape of Illinois. Just for a second they smelled sweet and inviting, but then she smelled the stale cigar odor that permeated the house and the pies smelled like bait.

Annie stepped into the living room and saw her mother sitting on the sofa, staring into space. Annie thought she resembled the deer head mounted above her. And why not? Both were victims—trophies of her father. She moved across the room, closer to her mother. "Mom."

Her mother did not respond.

"Mother? How are you doing?"

Her mother looked up at her sharply. The two women's eyes met. There was something different in her mother's eyes. Hatred, Annie suspected.

"I see you kept your promise, Annie," her mother said coldly, then walked into her bedroom and closed the door.

"Oh, see what I mean, Sweetie, your mother just isn't herself. Well, it's no wonder, really. After forty years of marriage, then to suddenly lose your husband with no warning at all—"

Annie interrupted her aunt, "Does she still keep the liquor in here?" Annie opened the antique oak ice box in the den, found the Tanqueray and vermouth, retrieved some ice, expertly shook the tumbler and poured herself a large martini. "Any olives in there, Salmon?" She could feel her aunt's disapproval. "It's okay, Salmon Patti. Dad himself invited me to drink with him the last time I was home," she added sarcastically.

Annie settled in her father's well-worn chair and

Patti excused herself to take a little nap.

"Free, White, and over twenty-one," Annie said to the deer head staring at her. "Those are the words, among others, that he used to describe me the last time I was home."

Last Christmas, when she and her father were alone, he sat in this chair and prodded her once again about what she knew of Sarah's disappearance. He rolled the cigar around in his mouth and leaned across the coffee table toward her. She remembered his colorless eyes narrowing to slits and the corners of his stained lips turned upward in a sneer. "So are you a dyke, or what?" he asked.

That's when she threw the martini at him and left with her now famous last words.

After that thought, she had to get out of the house. She couldn't stay there. Her mother wasn't talking to her, and Annie's presence obviously made her more upset.

You can't keep running away, Annie.

"Watch me, Sarah."

Just as she walked out the back door, her brother, Bud, drove up in Ruby. The red truck gave her the willies. Bud hopped out of the truck and greeted his sister with a little hug even though they were anything but close.

"Annie, there's someone I want you to meet. This is my fiancée, Gwen." Bud appeared nervous, shifting his weight from foot to foot.

Annie stepped back from her brother's hug just as Gwen was climbing down out of the truck. "Fiancée … I didn't know." Annie turned to greet the woman who would soon be her sister-in-law. "I'll bet we have a lot to talk about."

Bud's surprise revelation that he was engaged to a Black woman was a pleasant distraction for Annie. She thought about how their father would have responded to his only son planning to make grandchildren with a "darkie." Obviously, dear old Dad didn't know about Gwen. Maybe Bud wasn't a hopeless case after all.

Annie wondered if Gwen recognized how dysfunctional this family was. Did she realize that most people don't announce their engagements the day after their father's death? Did she realize that most people aren't physically sickened by childhood memories? Annie was sure that most people don't have conversations with ghosts, either, but that was a secret she hadn't even shared with her shrink.

Bud tucked Gwen's hand safely in the crook of his arm as if nothing unusual was happening and turned to go inside. His eyes questioned Annie about why she was hesitating by her car.

Annie couldn't gauge whether her mother already knew about Gwen, but didn't wish to be present for the confirmation. "Since you guys are here to be with Mom, I need to run over to Jayne's. See you later, Bud."

Gwen looked at Bud and shrugged as Annie backed the Dynasty out of the drive.

There weren't too many places to run in Dodge. Her car found its way to Jayne's mother's driveway, and she sat there for a while hoping no one would notice her. She found herself staring out into the back yard, which had shrunk since they were kids. But the three cherry trees were still there. She swung open the door of the car and walked out to the trees. She could smell the cherries ripening and a wave of nostalgia swept through her like cool water. It seemed Jayne, Mebo and Annie spent most of their childhood in the trees in Jayne's back yard. Certainly, Annie's back yard would not have been a good place to play.

At a very young age the girls named the trees Baby Tree, Main Office and Devil Tree. Baby Tree was for little kids and kids who couldn't climb trees very well; Devil Tree was for kids they didn't especially like; and of course, Main Office was where Mebo, Jayne and Annie had their offices. When the cherries were ripe they sat up in their offices and stuffed themselves with the tart, red fruit, spitting the pits at each other.

Annie guessed they were about eight when Jayne's father built the Triangle Tree House in an ancient apple tree at the very back of Jayne's yard. It overlooked Chet's lot to the east and was directly over the roof of the Little House. The Little House was an old goat barn that they had turned into a play house when they were seven. Jayne's mother used to bring Dixie cups of lemonade and cookies out to the trees and dubbed the girls The Three. They were together every available minute. They lived in the world of trees in Jayne's back yard until they went to junior high.

Looking back, it was easy for Annie to see that they should never have given up trees for boys.

Annie stood there holding onto a branch of the Main Office and tried to regain some of the little girl who spent so much time up there so many years ago. She couldn't even see the stump of the apple tree. Some things just disappear.

"Annie, Annie, what are you doing out here?" Jayne hurried toward her friend with her arms outstretched. Old friends embraced. "Spent a lot of time in these trees, didn't we?"

Annie pulled away from her friend and became a 38 year-old publisher again. She wondered why she always did that. She pulled away when she needed to be close. Her shrink said it was because she learned at a young age not to trust. Annie thought if she couldn't trust Jayne, she must be hopeless. Jayne, who had never hurt or abandoned her. Even now, when she lived half-way across the country, they kept in touch by phone and letters. Jayne, who had dropped everything and put her struggling practice on hold, came to hold her hand at her father's funeral. But Jayne wasn't the only one who had never hurt her. There was Mebo, too. Mebo had never hurt her and had tried to stay in touch.

"Why am I still so angry with her? Why didn't I ever answer her letters? Guilt," thought Annie.

"I'm sorry about your dad, Annie." Jayne put her hand gently on Annie's shoulder. "How's your mom doing?"

"She's a train wreck, as usual, Jayne," Annie replied lightly. "Oh, and guess who's coming to the funeral," Annie winked. "I just met my sister-in-law-to-be. Obviously, Dad had never met her. She's Black. Can you imagine?"

Jayne just shook her head sarcastically, "Your dad would have *really* liked that. Listen, Mom and I were just sitting down to lunch, and she'll be so happy to see you again. Come on in and join us."

Stand by Me

BEN E. KING

No, I won't be afraid,
No I won't be afraid
Just as long as you stand,
Stand by me.

"Mom, look who's here."

Her mother's arms encircled both of them and she enveloped them with her laugh. She held on to them until Annie melted and hugged back a little. "You girls! It's about time I had you both in this kitchen again. Sit down. I'll just get another plate. You need to eat, Annie. You look thin to me. But you still look as pretty as ever. I was so sorry to hear about your dad. We were all just shocked."

Annie tried to be polite and picked at her chicken salad, but Jayne could tell she was preoccupied. Jayne's mom must have known something was up, because she barely finished her lunch when she announced that she had to run up to the Square for something.

"I like the way your mom's house feels. I feel like a little girl here, the way little girls are supposed to feel. Safe and loved." Annie was looking through the window to the back yard, "I think this is the only place I ever felt that way. This house and Mebo's house." Her thoughts trailed off. She looked at Jayne.

Jayne had stopped eating and was listening intently.

"Jayne, I want to stay here with you and your mother this weekend."

"Well, sure you can, but what about your mother? I thought you probably—"

Annie interrupted, this time crying, "I won't—I can't stay in that house! Mom won't even talk to me. I know that somehow she thinks this is all my fault."

"Oh, I doubt that, Annie, but you know you're always welcome here. Whatever is best." Jayne was surprised at Annie's show of emotions. She usually kept things inside her.

"Look," Annie pleaded, wiping her eyes, "can we just go back out to the cherry trees for a while? I think I need to sit in my office."

"Well, if we're going to climb trees you'd better get some jeans on. Where is your suitcase?"

Outside, Annie tried very hard to be a little girl again, and as usual, she accomplished what she set out to do. They struggled into the Main Office, giggling like nine year olds, eating cherries, and spitting pits at each other.

Jayne's foot slipped and she nearly tumbled from the tree. "Why is it so much harder to climb these trees than it used to be?"

Annie thought about the question and answered

with a mouth full of cherries, "Because we know about falling now. Until you screw something up and fall flat on your face, you don't think about getting hurt."

Their eyes met through the branches. The playful mood was harder to hold onto now. Both women knew that they were talking about Sarah.

The branch Jayne was sitting on, her office, broke with a loud crack, and she landed on the ground under the tree in a shower of cherries.

Annie jumped down from her office. "Are you okay, Jayne? God, you look, uh, you look …"

Jayne rubbed her rear and checked her feet and legs for scrapes and bruises. Both women began laughing. The laughter broke through the carefully constructed boundaries Annie had erected around her emotions. She laughed so hard that she fell to the ground beside her friend. It was contagious, and soon Jayne was laughing as hard as Annie, holding her stomach.

"Stop, stop, Jayne!" Annie was barely able to get the words out. "I'm serious, I'm going to pee my pants." Annie tried to catch her breath and will herself more bladder control. She wondered why it was that she never heard of anyone else actually laughing until they wet themselves. Was it really only The Three who ever laughed so hard?

"Look!" Jayne puffed out the word and pointed to the street where Bud and Gwen had pulled Ruby over and were jumping out of the truck. "They probably think we're dying here."

The laughter convulsed them, and Annie lost bladder control. She couldn't catch her breath. She was on her back, still laughing when her brother's concerned face blocked out the sun.

"It's okay, Bud, Jayne just fell out of the tree," Annie said with feigned seriousness.

"Damnit, Annie! Dad's been dead a whole day and a half. Try not to take it so hard. Come on. You need to get back to the house and get cleaned up. We've got to go to the funeral home and make the arrangements."

"Arrangements? Surely that's all been taken care of." Annie stood up and tried to brush the grass off her wet jeans. It felt strange to her to be so serious so soon after wetting her pants.

"No, it hasn't all been taken care of," Bud's face was red as he spoke. "For once you'll have to act like part of this family!"

Gwen just stood behind him looking at the ground. The situation was stiff with tension.

Jayne winced with pain as she stood up and brushed off her clothes.

"Hi, I'm Jayne Lipton, Annie's friend from way back. You must be Bud's fiancée." Jayne graciously reached her hand toward Gwen. The Smoother of Conflicts, Annie had called her.

Gwen smiled, and a look of relief appeared on her face for a second, then she looked to Bud to read his face and see how she should respond. Bud was still stern, and he was trying hard to look indignant.

The interaction wasn't missed by Annie.

"Come on, Annie. Get home and get changed." The disgust was clear on Bud's face.

"Bud, I'm staying here tonight. My suitcase is already in the house." Annie fortified herself for the rebellion. "Mom's house is too crowded with you and Aunt Patti there, and I feel more comfortable here anyway."

"Well, shit, Annie!" Bud stormed back toward the truck and gave a backward glance to Gwen, who obediently followed. "Meet me at the Holvey Funeral Home in fifteen minutes."

Jayne and Annie looked at each other in silence until Ruby had pulled away from the curb.

"My God, they are just like a young Mom and Dad, only in color," said Annie shaking her head in disbelief.

Annie's thighs were already starting to chafe from her wet jeans. She stopped trying to pull the denim away from her legs and grimaced at Jayne. In a second they, one sore and one wet, were laughing and hobbling toward the house.

Great Pretender

PLATTERS

Oh yes, I'm the great pretender.

Annie ran up the stairs in Jayne's house and grabbed her tote bag. The laughter had changed to anxiety as she hurried to get ready to meet Bud at the funeral home. She started the shower and set to work pulling off the jeans that were sticking to her legs. Steam filled the room, clouding the full-length mirror that covered the wall opposite the shower. She sat bent over on the stool and rummaged in her tote looking for her shampoo and conditioner. "Why is it," she thought, "after so many years of business trips, I still don't know how to pack?" Finally, she turned the tote upside down, dumping its contents on the floor.

When she located the items, she stood and realized that the fog nearer the ceiling was much denser than it was nearer the floor. She suddenly felt dizzy and thought she must have stood up too quickly. She reached out to the mirror to steady herself. Her naked reflection in the mirror was blurred by the steam and looked vague and fuzzy. She thought that was the way she often felt lately—unrecognizable.

But I still know you, Annie.

HELL OUTTA DODGE   33

Annie swallowed a scream as she jumped back from
the mirror. She opened the door to Jayne's room to let
the steam flow out. Jayne was just walking into the
room and froze when she saw her naked friend standing in the door to the bathroom, shivering.

"What's wrong, Annie?" Jayne was worried.

"Oh, nothing really. Just too much steam," Annie
laughed a little to let Jayne know that everything was
okay, and grabbed a towel to cover herself. "And, as
usual, I'm rushing too much. Do you mind if I leave the
door open? The steam bothers me."

"Sure, leave it open," Jayne said, reassured. "Just
take it easy, Annie, you've been through a lot lately."

As she stepped into the shower, Annie remembered
all the times when they were growing up that she convinced Jayne and Mebo that there was nothing wrong.

What Annie didn't know about packing, she made
up for in speed dressing. She was barely five minutes
late when she arrived at the funeral home. Bud and
Gwen were waiting for her at the door, and Annie could
tell by the calm look on Bud's face that they hadn't
been waiting long.

Annie let Bud make the final decisions about the
funeral. She really didn't care what urn his ashes were
placed in or what music was played at the funeral. Mr.
Holvey, the funeral director, was solemn and grave, the
way only funeral directors can be. Ever-present Gwen
sat silently next to Bud during the whole thing.

Bud had brought their father's gray suit in. He decided on the casket, pall bearers, even the flowers. Annie just sat there and nodded in agreement whenever Mr. Holvey looked at her.

Annie wasn't sad or happy or anything really, except remotely interested in all the decisions required in order to have a funeral.

Only an hour and a half ago, she was rushing through a shower and pulling on a deep green business suit. Now she sat in the depressingly appointed office of J. J. Holvey Funeral Home, watching her little brother become the man of the family. She never got a chance to ask him if their mother knew about his engagement. With Francis Leslie McDonald out of the picture, Annie felt sure that Bud would feel free to do anything he wanted without a care about what their mother thought.

The wake would be tonight. Annie tried to picture what it would be like. The family would stand in a line beside the open casket and people would file by them, shake their hands, and hug them. Organ music would provide a moaning background for people's hollow condolences. Sprays of funeral flowers, gladioli and carnations would clutter the room.

She tried to imagine what her father would look like lying in the bronze-tone casket. She imagined him there with his balding head propped on a puckered white satin pillow and those thick-callused hands folded over his bloated chest. She wondered if his nose would be as red and swollen-looking as it had been in life.

Mr. Holvey droned on as she pictured all of this. She could see her mother standing over the casket, crying, and her father reaching into his pocket, producing a cigar. Then she saw her mother flick a lighter and light his cigar for him. Her mother wouldn't miss a tear as the room filled with his cigar smoke.

"You pervert," Annie muttered under her breath.

"Pardon me?" said Mr. Holvey.

Annie jerked her eyes away from the pink shade of the torchiere she had been staring at and looked at her brother who was staring at her.

"What did you say, Annie?" asked Bud innocently.

Gwen was looking at her with concern.

"Nothing. No. I'm afraid this is all too much for me," whispered Annie.

Bud seemed to approve of Annie's answer and returned his attention to Mr. Holvey.

"So, the family should be here by six tonight, and friends will come to pay their last respects at seven," Mr. Holvey continued.

Annie tried to keep from laughing when she pictured people "paying respects" to her father. Then Bud stood and shook Mr. Holvey's hand. He reached for Annie's arm to help her up and gave a backward glance to Gwen that said, "Come, girl, heel."

Outside the funeral home, Bud was gentle with his sister. He took her earlier comment to be the confused product of deep grief, and he respected that. Annie was glad that the comment hadn't slipped out any more clearly than it had.

"Annie, I think you should come by Mom's house for a few minutes," said Bud as he closed the car door behind her.

"Do you, Bud?" asked a hopeful Annie, "Do you think Mom will talk to me now?"

"Ah, Annie, she's just upset. She knows you really didn't mean what you said last Christmas," urged Bud.

"She does, huh? Well, I'll stop by for a little while. Then I'll have to get back to Jayne's and get ready for the visitation. I'll follow you over there."

Annie waited for Bud and Gwen to drive about half a block before she started in after them. When she knew they were too far away to see her clearly in their rear view mirror, she burst out in laughter.

"That *asshole!* That *perverted*, screwed-up, son-of-a-bitch!" Her laughter mixed with rage and it came out in tears. A block from her mother's house she parked on the shoulder to collect herself. Bud and Gwen waited in the driveway for Annie to catch up with them.

"Are you okay, Annie?" asked Bud.

"Yeah, I'm okay" she answered. "Let's go in and see how mom is doing."

Their mother met them at the door with a question on her face.

"Everything's taken care of, Mom," said Bud. "We're to be back at the funeral home tonight by six."

"How are you doing, Mom?" asked Annie.

"Oh, Annie," her mom said through tears, throwing her arms around her daughter. Her mother's cheek was soft and wet against Annie's. For a moment she felt her mother's loss and her eyes filled with tears.

"It will be okay, Mom," whispered Annie.

Her mom tried to catch her breath. Annie led her mother to the couch where they sat quietly. Annie patted her mother's wrinkled hand. She looked up to see Aunt Patti standing in the doorway, dabbing at her eyes with a crumpled tissue.

"Did Bud tell you that I'm going to stay at Jayne's?" Annie asked her mother gently.

Her mother nodded and squeezed her daughter's hand.

"Do you want me to help you get ready for the wake tonight? I could go get ready and come back to help you," said Annie.

"No, Dear, that's okay," her mother sniffled. "Your Aunt Patti can help me. You run along."

Annie hugged her mother and said good-bye. "I'll see you at six."

Dreams of the Everyday Housewife

GLEN CAMPBELL

Oh, such are the dreams
of the everyday housewife

Mebo looked around at her house. Bella was still working on the laundry, but Betsy was helping her fold, and Mebo couldn't remember the last time the house looked so clean.

Mebo knew that the twins worried about the way she talked to herself. They probably thought she was crazy. Why wouldn't they? They certainly heard their father call her that often enough. Mebo felt she relied on the twins more than she should. After all, they were just sixteen. But she didn't have anyone else to rely on or talk to. As close as she felt to the twins, she still couldn't explain about Sarah.

How could she explain something she didn't understand? Mebo didn't know why Sarah talked to her whenever Jayne or Annie were near. It made her feel crazy, not because she heard Sarah's voice inside her head, but because she didn't understand why Sarah should be talking to her at all. She and Sarah hadn't even been that close.

Trying to figure this out always gave Mebo a headache, and her head was really beginning to pound when the phone rang.

"It's for you, Mom, it's Jayne," Bella called from the kitchen and went back to the laundry.

"Mebo! I got to my mom's this morning. Annie is going to stay at my house, can you believe it? It will be like old times. We'll probably drive Mom nuts. She and Bud just went to make arrangements for the funeral." Jayne spoke in a flood of words.

"Jayne, it's good to hear you. You talk like you always did—non-stop! Why don't you drive out here for a cup of coffee?" She hoped she sounded calmer than she felt.

"Sounds good, I'll see you in a little while." Mebo hung up before Jayne could even say good-bye. Immediately, a rush of anxiety shot through her body. Jayne was coming to her old, dingy farm house. Mebo longed for her new house—the house whose remains lay black and morbid not 100 feet away from where she sat.

"It's evil," Mebo whispered to herself. She shivered as she did whenever she allowed herself to remember the fire last summer. They never caught the handsome, young farm hand who had become such a part of their lives and who disappeared the night of the fire. She could still smell the stifling, chemical stench when she thought about it. The fire took almost everything they had, including most of Mebo's hope for a better future.

Jayne had visited a couple of times before when she had come back to Dodge to visit her parents, and each time Mebo felt embarrassed by the humble house cluttered with children's things. Each time the "Sarah spells," as she thought of them, increased. Mebo believed if only she had her new house she wouldn't feel so inadequate. With her new house, perhaps she wouldn't feel as if Jayne and Annie pitied her for living near Dodge with her high school sweetheart and a house full of children. She thought maybe then the Sarah spells would go away too, although she didn't know why that would be. Then, as always, when she attributed those feelings to Jayne and Annie, she got angry at them.

"At least I have a husband," Mebo hissed under her breath. Then just as quickly as the anger appeared it was replace by guilt, and Mebo felt miserable again. She hoped that Bob would stay in the field while Jayne was there, then felt another twinge of guilt for thinking that.

She started to make the coffee when Benny yelled, "Ma, Belinda crapped all over the floor! Ooohh, *gross-out!*"

Belinda was screaming by the time Mebo left the coffee maker and headed for the living room. She stood in the doorway looking at the room that had been so clean only minutes before. The floor in front of the television was smeared with feces, and Belinda was covered in it. Benny ran to the bathroom gagging.

"Betsy, Bella, help me!" Mebo was panicking.

"Chill out, Mom," Betsy arrived at the scene first. "It's just baby crap."

Bella appeared with a towel that she wrapped around her baby sister and headed for the bathroom. Betsy grabbed the paper towels and a can of Woolite carpet cleaner and went to work. They ignored their mother who was sitting in the rocking chair crying into her hands.

By the time Jayne pulled up a few minutes later, Belinda was happy and bathed, and all that remained of the catastrophe was some damp carpet and the smell of Lysol. Mebo ducked into the bathroom, wiped her face and ran a comb through her hair, then went to the door to meet Jayne.

Stand by Your Man

TAMMY WYNETTE

Sometimes it's hard to be a woman,
Giving all your love to just one man.

"Jayne, you look so good!" Mebo hugged her friend in the doorway. Jayne was wearing a short, denim skirt and a T-shirt with a hand-painted pastel design. Jayne looked prettier than she ever had in high school. She had a style of her own now and she seemed more self-confident. Her sable, chin-length hair bounced as she moved.

Mebo had put on some clean blue jeans and a Dodge Darts T-shirt before Jayne came. Now she was painfully aware of the way she must look to Jayne. She had gained 40 pounds since high school and hadn't even thought about putting on makeup in years. Her long, red hair was streaked with gray and pulled back in a ponytail. She led her friend into the living room.

"The whole gang's here," Mebo announced to Jayne. "You remember my kids. These two young ladies are Betsy and Bella."

The twins were obviously impressed with the way Jayne looked as they said hello.

"This tall boy is Brad. He's twelve. Doesn't he look

like Bob?" She didn't wait for Jayne to respond. "This is Benny, who just turned six," Mebo explained as she stepped behind him and rested her hands on his shoulders.

Benny scowled and twisted away from his mother.

"And this little goober," Mebo reached down and retrieved Belinda from the playpen, "is Beebee."

The baby squealed and smiled at her mother and Jayne.

"Actually, her name is Belinda, but she's been Beebee ever since we brought her home from the hospital."

"Oh, she's a doll, Mebo." Jayne cooed at the fat baby and took her from her mother. "Hi, Beebee."

Bella grabbed Betsy's arm and squealed with delight. Brad tossed a throw pillow at this mom as he said, "Think fast, *Mebo*."

Betsy continued laughing, "I can't believe people really call you *Mebo*. How lame!"

"Hey, Mebo's her name," Jayne said with mock seriousness. "None of this Briget stuff for The Three."

"The Three!" squeaked Bella as she and Betsy crumpled to the floor in laughter.

"Stop, Bella, or we'll pee our pants again," cried Betsy.

"*Pee. Your. Pants.* I can't believe it!" Jayne rolled her eyes. "Must be genetic." She stood holding Beebee, bouncing her gently, while surveying the room full of laughing children. "You've got some good-looking kids, Mebo. You and Bob must be very proud. They've grown

so much since I saw them last, and the baby is dar-
ling."

Mebo collected the baby and put her back in the
playpen.

"Come on in the kitchen. I think I promised you
some coffee." Mebo forgot about feeling frumpy. She
was proud of her kids and, obviously, Jayne was impressed with them. Maybe even a little envious.

Jayne sat down at the huge, orange Formica table
while Mebo poured coffee into green and yellow John
Deere mugs. She put a pan of brownies on the table in
front of them.

The kitchen carpet was a riot of orange and browns.
The colors were darker under the chairs where years
of spilled Kool-Aid had stained it. The butcher block
Formica counter was cluttered with small appliances
and ceramic canisters shaped like giant mushrooms
with gold-colored butterflies for handles. The harvest
gold refrigerator was covered with school papers and
pictures the kids had drawn.

"How's Annie taking her father's death?" Mebo
asked as she cut the brownies. "She was probably really shocked, huh?"

"Well, she's pretty emotional right now, but I think
she'll be all right. I hope we can all get together this
weekend."

Mebo ignored the implication that she and Annie
should mend fences. She didn't even know why Annie
turned so cool toward her so many years ago.

"Did your mom tell you how Mr. McDonald died?" Mebo plopped her elbows on the table and leaned toward her friend.

Jayne shook her head.

"It was really weird. Bob says he thinks it was because he found out about that Black girl that Bud's been seeing. Anyway, he drove to the plant Wednesday morning and parked in two parking places ... so his truck wouldn't get dinged up. What did he call that truck?"

"Ruby," Jayne answered through a bite of brownie.

"Yeah, Ruby. Strange man." Mebo continued, "Anyway, he got out and locked the door and just as he was waving to Shorty Shubert across the parking lot, he just keeled over. Shorty said he was dead before he hit the pavement." Mebo whispered and shook her head to emphasize the importance of the information, "Hadn't been sick or anything."

"Mean and sick in the head maybe, but not *sick* sick," Jayne said.

"I guess," agreed Mebo.

"So you knew that Bud was seeing a Black girl?" asked Jayne as she got up to pour herself another cup of coffee.

"Oh, yeah, I think everyone in town knows. It wouldn't be any big deal if Butch McDonald weren't his daddy. He was never very open-minded."

"I guess that's an understatement!" Jayne laughed and smiled knowingly at her friend. "Oh, I met her."

"Met who?" asked Mebo.

"Bud's girlfriend—fiancée, actually," Jayne continued.

"Fiancée!" Mebo almost yelled the word. "Fiancée?" she whispered. "You mean to tell me that they announced their engagement right before his dad's funeral!"

"Well, I guess so. But I don't think Butch was too much of a stickler for social etiquette, anyway." Jayne giggled into her coffee cup. "Do you know that his real name was *Francis Leslie*?"

"You are terrible!" Mebo started laughing with her. "Please, Mebo, don't get me started." Jayne was leaning across the table pleading with her friend. "Annie and I laughed so hard this morning that she wet her pants."

"Are you kiddin' me?" exclaimed Mebo with an undeniable Midwestern accent. "What were you doing? I can't imagine Annie doing that especially when her dad just died."

"Don't be hard on Annie, Meebs. She and her dad had a terrible relationship. He wasn't much of a father, you know. Anyway, it's natural for people's emotions to get out of control when something like this happens," explained Jayne.

"Well, I guess you'd know, being a therapist and all," Mebo said and winked.

Jayne wadded up her paper napkin and threw it at Mebo. "Don't start with me. This weekend I'm not a therapist. I'm tired of it. I don't want to have to analyze anybody," she laughed. "I left my Sigmund Freud Se-cret Decoder Ring at home." Jayne prepared herself for the conversation that she knew must follow the mention of her career.

"How is your new practice going, Jayne?" Mebo knew that this was a sensitive area for her friend, even though she didn't fully understand why.

"It's going fine." Jayne tried hard to sound matter-of-fact. "I've finally built up some good referral sources in Des Moines. It'll still take a while before this practice is as productive as the one in Minneapolis."

Silently, she added that she would never be as successful as she was before a young male client had accused her of sexual misconduct. She felt the too-familiar lump in her throat fall to the pit of her stomach. She knew she was lucky that she didn't lose her license permanently.

"I still don't get it," Mebo shook her head innocently.

This was really more than Jayne was prepared to get into. "Oh, Mebo, it's really sort of complicated and I really don't understand it all myself."

Jayne looked to the door with a sense of relief when the tractor roared in from the field. Mebo pulled back the ruffled, gingham curtains and peeked out the window. A worried look came over her face.

"What is it, Mebo? Is something wrong?" asked Jayne.

"No, not wrong. I guess Bob finished in the fields earlier than he thought he would. Now, you'll be able to say hello to him, too." Mebo smiled meekly.

"It's been a while since I've seen Bob. I imagine he keeps really busy out here. Does he like it?" Jayne asked, reaching for a question to reduce the tension that Bob's impending presence created.

"Like what?" Mebo asked, confused and distracted.

"Like his job, I mean, farming," Jayne replied.

"Well, I don't know," Mebo answered, still confused. "I guess he likes it alright."

She sat down looking perplexed and started fidgeting with her coffee cup.

"I never thought about whether or not he likes it. Is he supposed to like it?" Mebo was drawing circles in a little spill of coffee on the table.

Bob came through the door and startled Jayne with his piercing gray stare. His faded jeans were torn and dirty and his plaid shirt had grease-stained sleeves and several buttons missing. Bob lifted his grimy cap by the brim, smoothed down his hair with a dirty hand and returned his hat. He shifted his attention to his wife, "You didn't say anything about having company."

"Bob, you remember Jayne," Mebo fidgeted and there was a quiver in her voice.

"Hell, yes, I remember Jayne. God, Briget, you think I'm an idiot?" grunted Bob.

Jayne jumped in, "Hi, Bob. I just stopped by to see Mebo and your beautiful kids. How are you doing?"

A look of pride washed over Bob's face briefly when Jayne mentioned his children. "Get me a beer, Briget."

He turned back to Jayne, "I'm doing all right. What about yourself? Didn't Briget tell me that you're a shrink now? You must make a pretty good living doing that, huh?"

"Bob, really ..." Mebo reddened as she handed him a can of Milwaukee's Best.

"So, how is little Miss Annie Fannie? I always got along really good with her," he laughed and took several gulps from his beer, all the while staring at Jayne. "Does she still have the biggest bazooms in town?"

"Bob, *please* ..." Mebo wanted to die from embarrassment.

Jayne looked down at her cup of coffee.

Bob belched, "I'm taking a shower, now. Keep the kids out of the bathroom." He belched again and grabbed another beer from the refrigerator as he left the room laughing.

Mebo wished she could melt into the carpet and disappear forever. When she heard the shower turn on, she breathed, "I'm so sorry, Jayne. I don't know what to say."

"Oh, Meebs, forget it," Jayne said. "The Three have to get together this weekend. Let's see, the funeral is tomorrow at 1:00. Are you going to be there?"

"Yeah, but Bob probably won't be able to make it. There's a lot going on around here this time of year," she replied.

"I'm sure everyone will be going back to the McDonald's home after the funeral, but I'm not sure low long

Annie will be able to take that." Jayne rattled on, "Let's get together tomorrow evening, for sure, okay?"

"Are you sure Annie will want to see me?" asked Mebo. "I mean we haven't exactly been as close as we used to be."

"Of course she'll want to see you, Meebs," Jayne replied. "What happened between you two anyway?"

"I don't know. I really don't," Mebo's eyes were beginning to mist. "We didn't have a fight or anything. She just lives in a whole different world and she probably thinks I am just a stupid old farmer's wife."

"Oh, Mebo, of course she doesn't. You have five wonderful kids and you are doing just what you always wanted to do." Jayne tried to be comforting.

"Am I?" Mebo asked. She was drawing in the coffee on the table again. "I can't remember wanting this. It just sort of happened. It just seems like ..."

"Seems like what?" Jayne asked.

"Oh, never mind," she looked up at Jayne and forced a smile. "It's silly. Forget it."

Mebo got up from the table just as the sound of the shower stopped. She grabbed a sponge from the sink and started clearing the table nervously.

"Oh, my gosh. It's five o'clock," said Jayne. "I'd better get home. Mom will wonder what happened to me."

She stood up from the table and hugged her old friend.

"Bye, kids," Jayne called to the living room then turned to Mebo. "Tell Bob good-bye for me. I'll see you tomorrow at the funeral. And remember, tomorrow night is the First Annual Main Office Reunion."

"Oh, wow, The Main Office," Mebo smiled as the old memories flooded into her head. Then she glanced toward the bathroom and said, "I'll ask Bob ..." When her eyes met Jayne's again she said, "I'll *tell* Bob I'm going out with you two. It will be fun."

So Far Away

CAROLE KING

Long ago I reached for you
And there you stood,
Holding you again
Could only do me good.
Oh, how I wish I could!

Jayne heard Bob yelling for another beer as she walked to her car. It amazed her that the captain of the Dodge Darts football team could turn into such an obnoxious, beer-swilling jerk and saddened her that Mebo was stuck with such a loser.

When she pulled the car onto the highway she chided herself for assuming that Mebo was unhappy with Bob. After all, those things she told Mebo back in her kitchen were true. She did have five wonderful kids, and even though Mebo said she didn't remember it, she did always want to get married and have a family.

Jayne found her *The Best of the Moody Blues* CD and put it in. She sang along with the words, "I'm just a singer in a rock and roll band" and changed them to "I'm just a therapist who is not in her office ... Don't tell me." And reminded herself that she didn't have to cure anyone this weekend.

The Moody Blues always made Jayne think of Peter. He loved that band. Twenty years ago she pretended to like their music because Peter was so into them. Years later, long after Peter was out of the picture, she listened to their songs and found, much to her surprise, that she actually really liked them. Now, listening in her car in Dodge, she wondered if she liked the music or if she was just in love with the memories it brought her.

"Memories," she said softly. "You're in love with memories, that's all."

When Peter went away to college, Jayne was a senior at Dodge High. She really believed then that they would both get their degrees, get married and live happily ever after. Twenty years later she could still feel the shadow of pain left over from when he broke her heart.

There were a few memories that never failed to bring tears to Jayne's eyes. One was remembering the day before she left for college. Her dog, Chip, who had grown up with her, was very ill. It was as if Chip knew she was moving away and that it was the end of an era. Jayne knew that he was suffering, and though she had always thought it was cruel to put animals to sleep, Chip's pleading eyes made her change her mind. She knelt beside him and gently stroked his swollen body while tears dropped onto his grayed hair. When she tried to say good-bye, the words stuck in her throat. He looked at her for the last time with total trust, understanding and forgiveness in his eyes. She left him there resting under the trees and went in the house. She told her mother that Chip didn't want to suffer anymore and that she didn't ever want to hear about it again. Her mother kept her word.

Another memory that always made Jayne cry was of the day near the end of her senior year when Peter called from Ames. He told her that he'd decided he wasn't ready for a serious commitment and that he wanted to date other people. He reminded her that she would be going away to college soon and that she shouldn't tie herself down. It wouldn't be fair to either one of them. This would be a good time for them to experience what life had to offer.

Jayne truly believed that the only life she wanted to experience was life with Peter, but she agreed with him on the phone that day. She just couldn't believe that he used the trite, old don't-want-to-tie-ourselves-down line. Even after twenty years she was amazed that was the part that hurt the worst. She refused to let him know how she was dying inside. She felt like her life was over and Peter's had just begun.

Dodge came into view and she and the Moody Blues contemplated how strange life can be. She married Jack only a year after that phone call from Peter. By then she had convinced herself that real love, the passionate kind, the kind she thought existed between her and Peter, didn't really exist. She looked for a practical relationship and found Jack. They struggled through two miserable years as married college students. The relationship proved to be anything but practical—or maybe it was too practical. Anyway, the marriage ended unceremoniously. It felt as if it was all just a short, unpleasant dream.

Sometimes, she thought that it would have been better if Jack had been a real asshole. If he had only given her a smoking gun, some unarguable reason to divorce, she would have felt much better about the thing. At least she would have experienced passion. As it was, she was left to question the very existence of passionate love.

She had reframed her relationship with Peter as adolescent romantic fancies and hormones. And she was usually successful with that explanation. But sometimes, when she listened to certain songs or drove through Sigley, she felt a quiet little terror and wondered if she had been wrong.

What if passionate love really did exist, and she was somehow just incapable of experiencing it? What if you only got one chance at it and her chance was Peter? It was this self inquisition that she went through whenever she came back to Dodge—and the guilt-sourced voice of Sarah—that kept her visits few, short and far between.

She had been single for 18 years now, and though she had been close to marriage a couple of times, she always felt she would be settling again. She couldn't bring herself to make a commitment. Whenever she got close, she wondered what would happen if she and

Peter met *now* for the first time.

As she maneuvered through Dodge, she let the day-dream grow on its own and imagined Peter and her happily sharing a home and their careers. At the door of her mother's house, she removed herself from the reverie and back into the stoic sterility of professionalism that defined her.

"Don't be foolish," she chastised herself. "You don't know anything about Peter."

Oh, Pretty Woman

Roy Orbison

Pretty Woman,
I couldn't help but see,
Pretty Woman,
that you look lovely as can be.

Annie was sitting in an aqua chenille bathrobe at the dressing table in Jayne's old room when Jayne returned from Mebo's. Mrs. Lipton had redecorated the room a couple of years earlier. The walls were very pale pink and the carpet and bedspread were a deep burgundy. The furniture was the same white, French provincial suite that Jayne had when she was in high school.

"The room is great, Jayne," said Annie. "I feel pretty …" she sang as she brushed on some mascara.

"How did your day go, Annie? Was it really awful?" asked Jayne.

"No, not awful, really. Actually, it was kind of funny … but enough of that." Annie brushed aside the issue. "How about your day?"

"Well, it really was pretty interesting. I went out to see Mebo and her brood. She asked about you," Jayne smiled as she plopped down on one of the twin beds.

"So how are Mebo and Bob and their twenty-seven offspring?" asked Annie flatly without looking away from the mirror.

"It's five offspring. The kids are sweet and Bob is an unbelievable jerk," said Jayne. "I don't know how Mebo can keep from poisoning that bastard."

"So he hasn't changed, huh?" laughed Annie.

Jayne stood up and walked behind Annie and spoke to her reflection in the mirror, "He remembered your ta-tas."

"Oh, gawd! Did he say that in front of Mebo? What a fa-*laaaming* asshole!" said Annie when she finished putting on lipstick. "So what do you think?" Annie asked, "I'll keep the always-appropriate, understated black dress for the funeral, but should I wear the conservative gray pinstriped suit tonight, or should I throw on the hunter green again? Too bad I didn't bring any festive Hawaiian print."

Jayne studied the reflection and looked for a trace of grief. She found none.

"I think I'll just wear the hunter green again," said Annie. She stood up, slipped out of the robe and into the blouse that she'd draped over a bedpost.

"Mebo and I decided to have the First Annual Main Office Reunion tomorrow night! You'll be free sometime tomorrow evening, won't you?" Jayne willed her friend to like the idea.

"A First Annual *Main Office* Reunion," Annie drew out the words, as if to make sense of them. "A First

Annual Main Office Reunion," she repeated, faster this time. "Sure, why not? Couldn't let it happen without some righteous melons," Annie laughed and thrust her chest out dramatically. "I'll be ready for some serious play time by then."

Annie finished dressing and looked at herself approvingly in the mirror.

"Well, I'm ready," she said. "Do I look sufficiently mournful?"

"You look fine, Annie. Mom and I will come by the funeral home later. Are you sure you're alright?"

"Piece of cake," said Annie, and she picked up her purse and left for the funeral home.

Planning another party without me, Jayne?

"Can The Three ever do anything without you, Sarah?" Jayne slumped back down on the foot of the bed.

You Don't Own Me

LESLEY GORE

And don't tell me what to do,
And don't tell me what to say.

Mebo hurried and cleaned off the table as soon as everyone was done eating. "Girls, come and start the dishes. I've got to get ready to go to the funeral home," she said as she rushed around the kitchen putting things away.

"Where are you going?" called Bob from the living room.

The girls came into the kitchen. Mebo heard Bob belch again and wondered how many times a day he did that. She thought he might be responsible for the erosion of the ozone layer.

"Bring me a beer, Bridget," Bob demanded.

Mebo rolled her eyes, grabbed a beer out of the fridge and went into the living room.

"I'm going to Mr. McDonald's wake. I told you that." She thought about adding that she would also be going to the funeral tomorrow and out with Jayne and Annie tomorrow night, but she thought better of it. She decided to take it one step at a time.

"Well, who's gunna watch the kids?" Bob whined.

"The twins will be home and it won't hurt you to stay with the kids for an evening once in a while. Besides, I'll only be gone for a little bit," explained Mebo.

Bob was engrossed in the game he was watching on television. "Yeah, yeah, whatever," he muttered and turned up the volume.

Mebo went into their bedroom and opened the closet. She pulled out the olive suit she bought for Easter last year. Tomorrow she would wear the only dark-colored summer dress she had. She bought it two years ago for Jayne's dad's funeral.

She went into the bathroom, plugged in the twins' hot rollers and turned on the shower. After she got undressed she searched the bottom of the vanity until she found her old bag of makeup. The zipper on the stained vinyl bag was stuck half way open and it broke apart when she tugged at it. The lid had come off a lipstick and waxy red stuff was stuck to most of the other contents.

"What a mess," she said to herself and briefly looked at her reflection. The mirror was beginning to fog and she looked a little fuzzy around the edges.

What do you see, Mebo, or is it Briget? Do you see a cheerleader?

Mebo slammed her hands against the vanity and held her breath for a second. Then she shook her head and stepped into the shower.

Na Na, Hey Hey, Kiss Him Good-Bye

STEAM

Na na na na,
Na na na na,
Hey, hey,
Good-bye

The family had an hour together at the funeral home before visitation began. It was more than enough time. Annie held her mother's arm when they walked into the viewing room, but stopped in her tracks when she saw the casket.

"Bud," Annie looked at her brother and nodded toward their mother. Bud left Gwen's side and took his mother's arm from Annie, then walked slowly with her until they stood in front of the casket.

Patti came and stood beside Annie and patted her on the shoulder.

"Go ahead, Salmon. I just need to stand here for a while," whispered Annie.

Annie and Gwen remained in the back of the room and watched the rest of the family stand silently in front of the casket.

"You know," said Gwen cautiously, "my mother always said that a person just isn't dead to her unless she sees him in the casket."

It was the first time Annie had heard Gwen say so much. "Well, then," said Annie, "I'd better go look at the S.O.B." Annie started toward the casket.

A person isn't dead unless you see her in the casket.

"Not now, Sarah!" hissed Annie.

Aunt Patti turned around and looked when she heard Annie speak. But when she saw Annie walking toward them crying, she rushed back to comfort her.

The rest of the family was already seated. Annie didn't know how long she had been standing there alone staring at her father. But she knew she felt like a six year-old when she arrived at the casket, and now she felt like an adult.

She looked at his dark, thick hands and whispered, "You'll never touch me again."

She turned and sat down next to Gwen.

All You Need Is Love

BEATLES

Nothing you can say,
but you can learn how to play the game.
It's easy.

Jayne and her mother sat at the antique oak kitchen table overlooking the deck her father had built the summer before he died. The aroma of hazelnut coffee filled the Saturday morning air, and Jayne's mother had already run out to Devin's Sweet Shop on the Square to get the cinnamon buns that Jayne was so fond of. Jayne loved this kitchen. Annie was right, it was a place to come to feel safe and loved.

That's what I wanted, too.

Jayne jumped enough to spill her coffee a little.

Her mother didn't seem to notice. "Annie must be exhausted after last night, and today won't be easy for her, either. I'm glad she's sleeping in." Jayne's mom poured another cup of coffee. "I hope she had a good visit with her family last night after the wake, poor dear."

Jayne stirred some sugar into her coffee, "I think in

some ways this will be especially hard for Annie, since she and her father could never get along."

"Can I get you something else to eat, Dear?"

"No, Mom, I'm fine. I usually don't eat any breakfast."

"I'm going to resist the urge to tell you that you really should eat better." Her mother set her coffee cup down and leaned forward, "So tell me about the man in your life."

"Mother," Jayne responded to her mother's standard question with resignation, but this time she was a little more prepared.

"Well, after all," her mother continued, "there must be one." Jayne was glad that she'd planned a diversionary strategy.

"His name is Joseph. He's really ... well, wonderful."

Jayne watched her mother's face light up and felt a twinge of guilt for deceiving her. "He moved into the offices down the hall from mine. A dentist moved out of there, and Joseph's practice had really outgrown the suite he had in the Memorial Plaza. A lot of my friends use him as their pediatrician, but I had never met him until he moved into my building."

Her mother looked as though she could see Nirvana in her coffee cup and asked, "So, has he ever been married?"

"Mom, you're such a mother," she laughed. "No, he's never been married. He's really quite different."

"What's this? In love?" Annie asked from the kitchen door. "Is that with a capital L?"

"Good morning, Dear, sit down and I'll get you a cup of coffee," Jayne's mother cleared her place from the table with newfound vigor and poured Annie a cup. "How are you feeling?"

Annie sat down and rubbed her forehead. "I have a little headache. Do you have any aspirin?"

"I'll just go get you some," Jayne's mother said as she scurried out of the room.

"Oh, Jayne, I am *so* hung over," moaned Annie.

"You poor thing. Did you and Bud hit the bottle last night?" Jayne asked.

"Not exactly, but I drank enough for the both of us."

Mrs. Lipton returned with the aspirin, poured Annie a glass of juice, and said, "If you girls will excuse me for a little while, I have to run up to Claire's to get my hair washed and set. I'm sorry to leave you girls, but it's my regular appointment."

When her mother had left, Jayne got the juice out of the refrigerator and refilled Annie's glass.

"Even though it's far too early in the day for it, tell me about your Love," Annie forced a smile.

"He's everything I said ... and more."

Annie continued rubbing her head.

Jayne watched Annie closely for her reaction as she continued, "Joseph is gay."

Annie looked up in playful surprise.

"He's a really good friend. Actually, it was his idea that I tell Mom all about him ... well maybe not *all*

about him. Joseph said that if I threw Mom a little tid-
bit she might quit asking me about 'the man in my life'
for the rest of the visit. I think it worked."

"So, then," Annie picked up the gauntlet, whispering in conspiratorial tones, "*isn't* there a man in your
life ... I mean ... you know." Jayne shuffled her chair
closer to her friend.

"Really, Annie, there's certainly more to life than
sex. Besides," she said it as much to convince herself
as to convince Annie, "there really isn't room in my life
for another person right now." Jayne changed the subject, "So where were you drinking?"

Everyday People

SLY AND THE FAMILY STONE

And different strokes for different folks,
And so on, and so on ...

Annie drained her third glass of juice and rested her face in her hands. She set about telling her friend about the night before.

"I was at the lake. I went to The Bottle Shop and got a pint of Jack Daniels and drove out to the damn dam and got damn schnockered."

Jayne shook her head, "By yourself?"

Annie's face was resting on the cool surface of the table as she recited the litany.

"The wake," she explained, "progressed pretty much as I imagined it would, except that my father behaved himself and refrained from smoking a cigar. People paraded by the casket, shook hands, and offered sympathies. Bud decided that it wasn't a good time to formally announce his engagement, and so Gwen sat in the second row of chairs instead of standing with the family."

"I wondered about that," Jayne took a bite out of her cinnamon bun.

"It was funny watching people whispering among

themselves, trying to decide if Gwen was really Bud's girlfriend."

"Did you see the regulars?" Jayne asked.

"It was weird. I recognized some of the people. All of them seemed to know me. They knew that I wasn't married and had a job that had something to do with books. My father always referred to me as his old-maid daughter. Mom must have told people about the book part." Annie knew that in the eyes of both her parents she was an enormous failure. If she would have married some local boy and worked in the Dodge Public Library, she could have taken a place among Dodge's elite. But she had to go off to God-forsaken New York City, and make more money than her parents ever saw. That was a crime for which she wasn't ready to do time.

"So who'd you see?" Jayne prodded.

"It was uncanny. The more things change the more they stay the same—at least in Dodge. Jacobsen's Hardware was represented, only now it's Stevie Jacobsen since Oleg passed away. Did you know he died?"

"Yeah, I think Mom mentioned it," Jayne poured another cup of coffee.

"J.R. is running King's now, since his parents retired to New Mexico."

"Now, I didn't know that," Jayne replied.

"Dave Light was there with his mom. The sons take their fathers' places, and Dodge doesn't skip a beat."

Jayne nodded in agreement.

"Oh yeah, Julian Van Pelt came to pay his last respects. He wore the same, long, brown wool overcoat that he wore year-round twenty years ago. He walked up to me and said, 'Well, the population of Dodge is now an even 4,026' and moved on. I suppose it was the nicest thing he could think to say at the time."

"He must be about 200 years old by now," Jayne mused.

"And from the smell of him, he hasn't taken the coat off to bathe for a least the past hundred."

Jayne stood and removed an invisible hat from her head, held it over her heart, and with a deep and solemn voice announced, "Julian Van Pelt, historian and poet."

"Go ahead, laugh at him. Everyone does, but I think he's one of the most interesting people in Dodge," Annie chided.

Jayne hung her head and sat back down with a mock pout on her lips.

"If you must laugh at Dodge's finest, how about Peeping Tomkins? He and his wife were there."

"It's the *Honorable* Peeping Tomkins, now," Jayne snickered. "He's a judge!"

Annie just shook her head, "There are probably other towns that put up with such ambitious voyeurs, but I'll bet it's only Dodge that makes a guy like him a judge. It was very difficult to accept his condolences and his roving eyes without laughing."

The two laughed over their coffee. "And, of course, Wilbur and Wanda came," Annie continued. "They wouldn't miss a visitation."

Wilbur and Wanda lived in one of the shabby apartments above the Square and made their living washing windows, sweeping sidewalks, or scooping snow for the businesses there. Though they attended every wake, they never actually paraded through the lines and greeted the families. They just sat silently in the back row of chairs.

"I think they may have come for the air-conditioning of the funeral home. It would be sad," Annie reflected, "if they hadn't come. When the wake was over, I drove Mom and Patti home. They were both exhausted and were in bed within half an hour. I could tell that Gwen and Bud wanted to be alone, so I excused myself." Annie searched her friend's face to see if she was being satisfied by this sanitized version of the night before. The laughter and reminiscing seemed to have done the trick.

Red Red Wine

NEIL DIAMOND

I'd have sworn that with time
Thoughts of you would leave my head.
I was wrong, and I find
Just one thing makes me forget:
Red, red wine

The night of the wake was a beautiful summer night. By nine it was just getting dark and the stars were already filling the sky. Annie stood by the car and listened. She could hear sounds of the neighborhood closing down for the night. A mother called for her children who were playing kick-the-can in the field across the street. A dog barked somewhere down the block. Mr. Clark, next door, still had his lawn sprinkler running and it made a rhythmic, gentle patter. She could smell his sweet, freshly cut lawn. It was peaceful. She looked back at the house, unable in the dark to distinguish the new siding from the old. The living room window went dark.

She got in her car and drove. At first she planned to just drive around the lake one time. She was feeling nostalgic, and she and Mebo and Jayne had probably "done the lake" a hundred times when they were in high school. But on her way to the lake road, her car pulled into the parking lot of The Bottle Shop, and she realized that the Valium she'd taken before the visitation had worn off. "Thank you, car," she laughed with approval. She bought a pint and headed toward the lake.

She parked at the dam, moved the seat back and got comfortable. A slow, steady stream of cars full of teenagers drove by.

"Of course," she said to the bottle. "It's Friday night."

She pulled off her shoes and pantyhose and walked barefoot across the dam to a little grassy spot amid three trees and sat down. She could see the Dynasty from there and began counting the cars that drove by, taking a drink from the bottle for every car. She knew that the teenagers were curious, but she counted on them not being curious enough to come looking for a strange car's owner.

"You can take the girl out of Dodge, but you can't take Dodge out of the girl," she mused.

It was true that she needed no explanation of the culture, the rituals of Dodge. They were the same as when she was a little girl. Dodge was an island in time.

There were three basic occupations for a man in Dodge. He could farm, work at the power plant, or sell things to those who did. The women of Dodge also had three choices. They could be housewives, teachers or nurses. However, having a job outside the home was looked upon as an embarrassment to her husband.

In some ways, Annie thought it would be much easier to live in Dodge. There weren't so many complica-
tions—not so many decisions to make. All you had to
do to be a success in Dodge was play by the rules. The
rules were really quite simple: marry young, have children, never set foot outside the county line, and don't
think too much.

"It's definitely too late for me," she said to herself as
she took another swallow from the bottle. "I've broken
all the rules."

*Why are you getting drunk, Annie? Are you
waiting for* Bob?

The alcohol was doing its job.

"No, I was waiting for you, Sarah," Annie said calmly. "I want to know what the hell you want."

Annie waited for the answer. Two more cars drove
by on the road across the little lake.

"Listen to me, Sarah," she said as she put the cap
back on the bottle. "I was a screwed up kid. I didn't
mean to hurt you."

She waited.

"I was jealous to death of Mebo. *She* was the cheerleader. *She* was the queen. *She* was going steady with
Bob. All I got were her table scraps. Bob would take
Mebo home by curfew and then come out here and
meet me. I'd take him anyway I could get him, Sarah.
I had no pride." Annie's speech was a little slurred and
she was talking louder. "So when you came to me and
told me that he wanted to meet you—"

I trusted you, Annie.

"You shouldn't have, Sarah!" She was nearly shouting. She waited for a response and then continued in a quieter voice, "I was used to feeling dirty, Sarah. I guess I wanted you to feel dirty, too. I was already used. My father ... my father ..." Annie's stomach started to quiver, softly at first, and then harder as her shoulders quaked with sobbing. Her hands clawed into the ground and pulled at the grass. She finally gave herself up to grief.

Annie didn't know how long she had been lying there crying. As if they belonged to someone else, her hands patted little hills of pulled-up grass. She fell against a tree when she tried to stand. She wrapped her arms around the rough tree trunk. "It's okay, Tree. I'm just a drunk, crazy old maid from New York. Pay no mind to me."

Annie maneuvered her way across the dam and stood by the car. She threw the empty bottle into the black lake and drove back to town.

Crazy

PATSY CLINE

I'm crazy for trying,
I'm crazy for crying,
And I'm crazy for loving you.

"Briget, what's wrong with you?" barked Bob. "You haven't moved since I left this morning. Where's my lunch? It's almost 11:00."

"Is it really? It can't be that late already. Where did the morning go? Sorry, Bob, I have a headache. I'll get you something right away." Mebo hurried into the kitchen.

"Where are the girls? How come they're never home?" Bob asked.

"I sent them in to the grocery store. Belinda's sleeping, Benny's watching his Saturday morning cartoons, and Brad was out helping you. Now they're all accounted for," she said as she sliced some ham.

"Don't you use that tone with me. You on the rag or something? So, did you see little Annie Fannie last night at the funeral home?" asked Bob.

"Yes, I saw her, but I don't remember anybody ever calling her that. Just when did you come up with that name anyway?" Mebo was feeling a little braver than usual this morning.

"Hell, everybody called her that at school. Where were you?"

Mebo set plates of sliced ham and bread in front of him. She got a bowl of potato salad and some pickles out the refrigerator.

"Briget," Bob scolded, "Where's the mayonnaise?" He looked at her as if she had committed a major sin. "Grab me a beer out of there," he ordered while she was still at the refrigerator. With the mayo and beer in hand, Mebo wondered how long it would take her if she tried to murder Bob with cholesterol and alcohol.

The screen door slammed behind Brad, who strode into the kitchen, dropping mud from his boots with each step.

"Brad, get back out there and take those boots off!" screeched Mebo.

He turned without saying a word to do as he was told.

"Don't pay any attention to her, Brad, she's on the rag," Bob laughed.

Mebo heard her son laughing at her as he came back to the table, and something inside her snapped.

"I'm sick of this!" Mebo screamed. "I'm *sick* of your comments and your orders and your ..." she searched for the right word, "and your smell!"

Bob stopped chewing his sandwich and stared at her.

"And I'm going to Butch McDonald's funeral today

and then I'm going out with Annie and Jayne. *You* can take care of the kids. *You* can get your own damn supper. You can take a flying leap for all I care!" Mebo stormed out of the house. She didn't start shaking until she had driven half way to town. She pulled the car onto a gravel road and parked.

She was out of control. She couldn't believe she just talked to Bob that way. She had never done anything like that. Not out loud, anyway.

"Maybe I am crazy," she said to herself, "I scream at my husband and I talk to ghosts and I can't talk to Annie at her father's wake."

Last night she had gone into Holvey's Funeral Home fully intending to walk right up to Annie and her family and tell them how sorry she felt for their loss. She'd practiced the words in the car on the way to town. But when she got there, there was already a crowd at the funeral home.

She stood beside Wilbur and Wanda and observed her old friend. Annie looked too elegant. Her shoulder-length blond hair was as shiny as it was in high school, but it was stylishly cut now. Her deep green, tailored suit was perfectly accented by tasteful gold jewelry. She looked like someone in the *Cosmopolitan* magazine she bought at the grocery store last week and had hidden from Bob.

Looking at Annie, Mebo felt frumpier than usual. She couldn't walk up to the front of the room wearing that drab olive suit. She reasoned that there were so many people there that Annie wouldn't notice her absence. So she just went home.

"Now what am I going to do?" Mebo asked herself. She knew that Bob would be going back into the fields soon, and she decided that she'd get her clothes together and go in to the Liptons' house and get ready there. She thought that as scary as facing Annie would be, it would be easier than facing Bob.

Trouble in paradise? Is this any way for the homecoming queen to treat her football hero?

Mebo turned the car around and spun the tires on the loose gravel.

Dizzy

TOMMY ROE

Dizzy, I'm so dizzy!
My head is spinning
like a whirlpool—it never ends.

"Well, here we go again," Annie remarked as she stepped out of the bathroom with a towel wrapped around her. "It seems like only yesterday that we had to go through this funeral home bit. Oh, I guess it was yesterday. Today it's the tasteful black dress, right?"

"Annie, you don't have to be funny with me," Jayne said quietly. "I know this is a hard time for you."

Annie finished pulling on her slip and sank to the bed. "After eleven years of therapy, I really thought I was getting over all the terrible things he did to me. Then the S.O.B. died, and I just feel so ..." she studied the patterns on the carpet as if the answers were there. "I just feel so guilty. Do you think I'll ever get over this, Jayne?"

"Of course you will. It's never easy," Jayne reassured her.

Annie discovered a run in her only pair of black pantyhose, but continued to dress anyway. After all, it was only a funeral. She pulled on the black dress that she thought she probably would never wear again after today. As she put the finishing touches on her makeup, she watched Jayne carefully via the mirror. Annie had been calculating her next move from the moment Jayne had agreed to come back to Dodge this weekend. She had decided and changed her mind almost continuously since then. "Jayne, you're going to think I'm really crazy." Even as she spoke the words she was thinking that there was still time to change her mind. Then, as if she were deciding to sky-dive, she thought that if she couldn't trust Jayne, she might as well hang it up.

"I've always known you were crazy," Jayne laughed.

"No, but really, Jayne," she paused for a deep breath. "Sometimes I actually hear Sarah talking to me," Annie confessed.

Annie's words took Jayne's breath away.

"Oh my God," gasped Mebo who was standing in the doorway looking as if she'd seen a ghost.

Reunited

PEACHES & HERB

Reunited, and it feels so good.

Mebo felt awkward when she knocked on Mrs. Lipton's door, but as soon as Jayne's mother saw her, she wrapped her arms around Mebo and the fears disappeared.

"Oh, it's that Mebo! This is just like old times—all three of my girls back in the house," Jayne's mother went on. "Jayne and Annie are upstairs getting ready. Scoot on up there; they'll be so surprised."

Mrs. Lipton had put new, soft carpeting on the stairway, and Mebo climbed the steps silently. Annie and Jayne obviously didn't see her standing in the doorway when she heard Annie's confession.

Mebo felt as if all the really bad things, the things too terrible to tell anyone about, were crashing in on her. It was one thing for her to think she was losing her mind, but it was another thing indeed to think that Sarah actually did talk.

"What is going on?" cried Mebo as her knees buckled under her and she landed on the floor of Jayne's room.

"Mebo, what are you doing here?" Jayne knelt down

beside her.

"God, Meebs," Annie closed the door of the room, "What's wrong?"

"I must be going crazy," Mebo was crying, "I yelled at Bob and then I came here. I shouldn't have come. You have enough to worry about without stupid old Mebo butting in."

"Are you kidding, Mebo?" Jayne asked. "You aren't butting in. We're glad you're here."

Annie joined them, adding, "Yes, we *need* you here."

They sat on the floor and held each other. Mebo didn't feel intimidated by Annie any more. She was one of The Three again. Strength began to trickle in.

"You and Bob had a fight?" Jayne asked gently.

"Not exactly," Mebo was trying to quit sobbing. "I just couldn't stand his crude comments or his ordering me around anymore. I really let him have it." The gravity of what she had done began to sink in, and she visibly shook. "Oh, my gosh. He'll never forgive me."

"Ordering you around?" Annie shook her head in disbelief as she paced the burgundy carpet in front of her soggy friend. *"Ordering you around?"* Her eyes showed outrage. "Honey, if he ordered you around, he deserved whatever he got. He should be glad it wasn't me yelling at him."

As soon as she said it, Annie realized her mistake.

"I ... I only meant," Annie stuttered. Blood rushed to her face.

"Oh, it's okay, Annie. I know you used to see Bob our

senior year. He told me all about it. His version, anyway." Mebo was feeling more comfortable. "Of course, to hear him tell it, he laid every girl in school and they all thanked him for it."

Mebo was gaining strength with each minute. She felt like the rosary Benny brought home from catechism class that glowed in the dark after he held it under a bright light for a while. Jayne and Annie were her bright light.

Annie and Jayne looked at each other for a clue to show them how to react to Mebo's revelation.

"Thanked him for that? That's a joke!" Mebo let out an evil laugh.

"Mebo, I've never heard you like this," Jayne was amazed.

"Not in the past twenty years anyway," added Annie. "Welcome back, girl!"

"I know, I know," Mebo picked herself up off the floor and offered a hand to her friend. "I'm supposed to be Mrs. Bob Dorman, mother of the year, 38 year-old cheerleader. But 38 year-old cheerleaders don't talk to ghosts." She looked at them coyly, "Do they?"

"You, too?" Annie asked. "Sarah?"

Mebo nodded her head while staring at her shoes.

"This is really getting weird," Annie looked to Jayne for some explanation.

"It's not uncommon for people to think they see or hear someone who has died. Especially after some trauma," Jayne rationalized, sounding for the world like a therapist.

Annie interrupted, "Don't give me that psycho-babble. Don't you get it? Sarah has been talking to both of us! And besides, we don't know for sure that she's dead."

Jayne sank onto the bed. "Make that all three of us," she confessed. Her mouth had gone dry.

The three of them froze, trying to understand what was happening.

It was Mebo who broke the stillness. "We're running out of time here," she sounded frantic and relieved at the same time. "What are we going to do?"

Annie looked at her watch, "Oh, shit. I'm supposed to be at the funeral home in ten minutes."

"Okay, look. We are going to talk about this tonight in-depth when we have more time," Jayne was playing the problem-solver again. "But first things first. Let's do what we have to do right now, which is to get Annie to the funeral home and get Mebo dressed."

Annie hurried out the door. "Tonight," she called over her shoulder.

Amazing Grace

JUDY COLLINS

Through many dangers, toils and snares,
I have already come.

Jayne, her mother, and Mebo sat together at the funeral, two rows behind Annie and her family. There was a good turnout, though Jayne thought it may have been out of curiosity as much as out of respect.

Reverend Cole from the First Baptist Church officiated, even though Butch McDonald hadn't set foot inside a church since the day he got married. "A bunch of mumbo-jumbo" he called it and warned his wife not to give them any of his hard-earned money. Mrs. McDonald went to church faithfully. It was the only act of defiance in her married life.

It was obvious that Reverend Cole couldn't think of too many good things to say about Butch. In fact, it was obvious that he didn't really know the man. When he referred to Butch as Francis Leslie, Jayne nudged Mebo with her elbow and they both looked to the casket to see if Annie's dad would protest.

He didn't.

Mostly, the Reverend talked about what a fine wife and family Mr. McDonald had.

"As if he deserved them," Mebo whispered to Jayne.

Gladys Richardson, better known to Jayne and Mebo as Happy Butt, had taught piano to half the girls in Jayne's class at one time or another. She played "Amazing Grace" on the organ. Jayne wasn't sure how much grace God bestows on child molesters.

"Betsy and Bella took piano lessons from Happy Butt for two years," Mebo whispered.

Jayne thought about all of the funerals at Holvey's she had attended. Funerals were a big social event in Dodge. But, in the 20 years since she had lived away from Dodge, she hadn't been to a single funeral anywhere else, unless she counted the graveside service for her secretary's husband who had shot himself in their Volvo.

It seemed to Jayne that every time she talked to her mother on the phone, someone else from Dodge had died, usually from cancer. She puzzled over the fact that people seem to die in Dodge frequently, yet the town never seemed to change. "Maybe it's the water," she mused.

In spite of the air conditioning, it was hot in the funeral home. Revered Cole's sing-song voice made it difficult to concentrate. It occurred to her that the flowers at funerals always looked the same. She imagined that they were all made of plastic and silk, and that Mr. Holvey brought them out of a big storage room whenever there was a funeral.

Jayne was drawn out of her day dream by the sound

of Annie's Aunt Patti blowing her nose. It reminded Jayne of a duck call. Mebo started to giggle and tried to cover it up with a cough. Jayne knew that if she looked at Mebo then, she would have a hard time keeping a straight face. That was another strange thing about funerals. Jayne always had an urge to laugh during them, even when she was truly mourning.

Happy Butt began playing the organ again. This time it was "How Great Thou Art," and the pall bearers carried Butch down the aisle. Jayne remembered that he was to be cremated, and she was glad that they wouldn't have to prolong their plans to attend a graveside service. She immediately felt guilty for thinking that, but the guilt had long since subsided by the time she and Mebo reached the car.

We've Only Just Begun

THE CARPENTERS

We've only just begun
to live.

"Can you believe the way Annie's aunt blows her nose?" Mebo burst out as soon as she had dropped Jayne's mother off at her house and was finally alone with Jayne. "I thought I was going to lose it right then and there! And *Francis Leslie!* Somehow, I don't think Butch would rest well knowing that everyone in Dodge now knows his real name."

Jayne laughed, "They might as well put him in a pink casket!"

Mebo continued, "I don't think he would have liked anything about the funeral. Not his son sitting there with a Black girlfriend, not Reverend Cole doing the service, and certainly not religious organ music."

"I can't believe Happy Butt is still giving piano lessons. She must be a hundred and twelve," said Jayne.

"She's not *still* giving lessons," Mebo reached over and turned up the air conditioning and adjusted the vents so they blew on her face. "I said the girls *took* lessons from her. Glad Ass retired after two years of them."

Jayne parked the car along the street in the front of the McDonalds' house.

"That's another thing Butch wouldn't like," said Jayne, nodding toward Butch's red truck. "Bud and Gwen have been driving Ruby all over town—doing *who knows what*—since he died."

"That man was crazy about his truck." Mebo flipped down the visor on the passenger side and checked her hair in the mirror. "He took better care of Ruby than any of his family. That truck has to be at least 20 years old and there isn't a scratch on it."

The two of them walked past the front door and down the driveway. They tapped on the back door and walked into the kitchen.

Annie was sitting at the round table, tracing the pattern in the table cloth. She was pale, and Mebo noticed wrinkles on her forehead that she'd never noticed before. Annie looked up, and when she saw Mebo and Jayne, she rose and enveloped first Jayne then Mebo in her arms.

Mebo was surprised at how thin and bony Annie's arms felt. She could feel her friend trembling, and she held Annie tightly, instinctively patting her back.

Annie's mother came into the kitchen from the living room. She looked surprisingly well, Mebo thought.

"How nice of you two to come," she said smiling. "Now we have lots of food, and I want you to stay. I know it means so much to Annie."

Mrs. Clark from next door came in carrying a large casserole. Mr. Clark was right behind her with an angel food cake under a plastic dome.

"Excuse me, Honey, this is hot," she said as she nudged Mebo away from the counter. Mebo sat down beside Annie at the table, where she would be out of Mrs. Clark's way.

"Now, Polly, this is chicken casserole," the neighbor said to Mrs. McDonald matter-of-factly. "I've got two more of them over in my freezer for you. I don't imagine you'll feel much like cooking for a while." She gave her neighbor a practical hug. "I'll be over to check on you later. You just let me know if you need anything, you hear?"

"Thank you, Mabel," Mrs. McDonald whispered.

"Ben, put that cake down on the counter," Mrs. Clark said, as if she had to direct her husband's every move.

Mr. Clark did as he was told and followed his wife out the door with a discreet bow to Annie's mom. The Clarks acted as if they came to the McDonalds' house on a daily basis.

"How much chicken casserole does she think we'll eat, anyway?" Annie whispered to Mebo.

"Those people are the salt of the Earth," Mrs. McDonald announced to the group. Everyone nodded in agreement.

Patti took charge of setting up a buffet on the kitchen table. Annie led Jayne and Mebo out to the patio.

"Your mom looks like she's doing really well, Annie," Jayne commented.

"I think she's relieved that it's all over," said Annie. "The wake, the funeral, the marriage. She never once stood up to him, and you know something, I think she's going to get back at him now by being happy and doing whatever she wants."

"What do you mean?" Mebo asked quietly.

"I mean, like just now. Dad would never allow the Clarks in the house when he was here. He called Mr. Clark 'the pussy' and Mrs. Clark an old bat," Annie continued. "And on the way home, Mom said that she plans on giving Ruby to Bud and Gwen for a wedding present. Dad never even *met* Gwen. He was such a bigot that he would have killed Bud if he knew was dating a Black woman."

"How do you feel about all of that?" Jayne asked, seriously.

"You're being a therapist again," Mebo reminded her and the three of them laughed.

"I do mean it, though," Jayne asserted. "How d'you feel?"

"I think it's cool. I'm surprised, though, because I didn't know Mom had it in her. And I think it stinks," Annie's face grew pale and pained again. "Because if all this time she's been capable of standing up to him, why didn't she ever stand up for me?"

"He's dead now, Annie," Jayne rubbed Annie's back

gently. "That's the difference."

Patti called out the back door, "You girls come in now and get something to eat. Funerals always make people hungry."

"Yeah, I'm dying for some chicken casserole." Annie looped her arms through her friends' arms, and they went inside.

Like to Get to Know You

SPANKY & OUR GANG

Yes, I would like to get to know you,
if I could.

Mebo and Jayne returned to the Liptons' house, and Annie stayed at her mother's talking with Gwen and found that she really liked her. Gwen had a year of college left before earning a degree in special education. Annie thought wryly that her degree might help her deal with Bud. Gwen said they didn't plan on getting married until she found a teaching job, and that then they would probably live in a larger community.

So, Annie mused, Gwen and Bud planned to get the hell out of Dodge. Annie thought that was a sensible plan.

Aunt Patti was right. The funeral had made Annie hungry. She ate a second helping of Mrs. Clark's casserole and a piece of apple pie that someone had brought by earlier. Patti and a blue-haired lady from the Baptist Church cleaned everything up and served coffee.

Annie thought her mother was enjoying herself and couldn't remember the last time that happened. Annie felt the atmosphere of the house change. Three days dead and the sick, hateful force that had filled the house was fading. She allowed herself to enjoy the feeling as things settled down, then excused herself and drove to Jayne's.

Traces

Faded photographs,
Covered now with lines and creases.
Tickets torn in half,
Memories in bits and pieces.

Mrs. Lipton met Mebo and Jayne at the door. "How is Mrs. McDonald doing?" she asked.

"She's doing really well, Mom," Jayne answered as she kissed her mother on the cheek. "Annie thinks her mother is relieved to have the funeral over with."

"It is an exhausting process to go through," Mrs. Lipton said, knowingly. "I think I'll ask her out for lunch next week."

Jayne and Mebo sat in the kitchen with Mrs. Lipton, sipping tea, and filled her in on who was at the McDonalds' house. They told her about Bud and Gwen's engagement. They talked about her flowers and what she'd done with the house since the last time Mebo was there.

"Is Bob watching the kids today?" Mrs. Lipton asked innocently.

Mebo lost her smile and gave Jayne a pleading look.

"Mebo is planning on spending the whole day with

us, Mom," Jayne explained. "And her Bella and Betsy are *sixteen* now."

"Sixteen!" Mrs. Lipton sounded shocked. "How can that be? It seems like only yesterday when you two were getting your driver's licenses. I must be getting old."

"You'll never get old, Mrs. Lipton," Mebo assured her. "You're just the same sweetie you were when we were in high school."

"Oh, Mebo, you are so dear. Do your parents still like St. Louis?" She poured herself another cup of tea. Mebo and Jayne both shook their heads at her when she held up the pot, silently asking if they wanted more.

"They still love it. Dad is planning on retiring next year and they talk about moving back here," Mebo shook her head. "But I don't think they would really give up their friends and their house there."

The phone rang, and Jayne's mother went to answer it in the family room.

"I just had an inspiration," Jayne gushed. "Let's have a makeover party!"

"Wha—?" Mebo was suddenly pulled to her feet.

"Come on, this will be fun," Jayne insisted, towing her friend up the stairs.

"You mean, you do my make-up, and I do yours?"

"Now you're getting it." Jayne was possessed with this idea. "And for inspiration," Jayne disappeared in her closet and came out with four dusty Dodge High yearbooks, "Ta da!"

"You're nuts!" squealed Mebo as they plopped down on the floor amid the books. "1970, '71, '72."

"And the best is yet to be, 1973!" they cheered together.

Jayne opened the 1972 book, "Look at this, look at this. Girls' Choir. Do you believe we wore dresses that short? Gawd, we could touch bare thigh without bending over!"

"Look how long your hair was," Mebo exclaimed. She turned the page, "Oohh, the AV team. And th-th-th-there's J-J-Johnny Wh-Wh-What's His Name."

"Johnny Brimley," Jayne said calmly. "And he's a vice president at Nicholas Claymore, thank you very much."

"Oh, I'm sorry, Jayne. You always liked him didn't you?"

"He's a really nice guy." Jayne flipped to the back of the book and read, "To a really special friend. I know we'll always stay close. Best friends forever, Mebo."

"Wow, that's deep," Mebo said with mock seriousness. She picked up the 1973 book. "Let's see what I wrote in this one."

Jayne looked over her shoulder and they turned to the front of the book. The pages were blank. Mebo looked at her friend, puzzled.

"Oh yeah," said Jayne in a serious tone. "That was the year I became too mature for writing in yearbooks."

"I remember that. You recited a lot of poetry that year." Mebo shot her friend the peace sign and rolled back laughing.

Jayne returned the peace sign, "It was a far out year, man." She sprang up and pulled out the chair in front of the dressing table and motioned for Mebo to sit down. "Bring the books over here. You can look at them while I style your hair, and remember," she continued with a phony accent, "*If you dun't loook goood, I dun't loook goood.*"

Mebo sat.

Jayne ran downstairs and brought her mother's hot rollers back up with her. She opened her cosmetic case and took out a jar of cold cream and a tube of blue facial mask.

Mebo looked at the jars, and then at Jayne, with alarm.

"Trust me, Dahlink," Jayne said as she pulled Mebo's long, red hair back in a ponytail. "Here, smear this stuff all over your face and wipe it off with the tissues," Jayne ordered, plugging in the electric rollers.

While she was waiting for Mebo to get the goo off her face, Jayne flipped through their senior yearbook. "Oooh, Meebs," Jayne teased, "Look at this *sexy* cheerleader!"

"I was hot stuff, wasn't I?" Mebo touched the page gently with her one clean hand. "I just loved being a cheerleader." She turned the page and caught her breath, then slammed the book closed with a crack.

"What's wrong?" Jayne was startled by the sudden mood change.

"That picture," Mebo said dryly as the color drained out of her freshly cleaned face. She was staring flatly into the mirror.

Jayne took the book gently from Mebo and found the picture of the cheerleaders. Then she turned one page more. It was a double page of candid shots that were taken throughout the year. Near the bottom of the page was a picture of three, smiling teenagers. Mebo had her arms around Bob's waist. Bob had his right hand in devil horns behind her head. His left arm was around Sarah's neck and his fingers entwined in her long, raven hair.

Jayne felt an icy chill go through her body. She shivered. Then she calmly picked up the books and put them back in the closet. She closed the closet door tightly as if to keep the bad memories locked away.

"Come on, Meebs," Jayne said lightly. "Back to the task at hand. We have to become beautiful before we go out tonight."

Just Like a Woman

BOB DYLAN

But she breaks just like a little girl.

Annie was almost a block from Jayne's mother's house when she realized how much she was looking forward to a night out with Jayne and Mebo. She was anxious to wipe the last few hours from her memory.

"Oh, brain fart!" Annie said out loud. "What we're going to need tonight are some Touch & Goes." Her car did a 180-degree turn in the middle of the street and headed back to The Bottle Shop.

Mr. Kirland greeted her as she entered. Annie wondered if he remembered her from last night.

"I need a fifth of cheap gin, a twelve pack of Coors and two big bottles of Squirt." Annie grabbed two bags of beer nuts off the counter.

"Have a nice night, ma'am," Mr. Kirland called to her as she left.

"I fully intend to, sir, thanks." Annie hated it when people called her ma'am. She was out the door like a shot.

Annie struggled with the bag of goodies while she opened the Liptons' front door. She looked around the vacant living room and hurried upstairs before Jayne's mother saw her.

"Hello ladies and germs," Annie giggled as she sprang into Jayne's room. "What in the hell are you doing?" she laughed.

Mebo and Jayne were sitting on the floor with their hair tied back. Their faces were covered in blue facial masks.

"You look like a couple of Smurfs!"

"We're having a makeover party," explained Mebo. "Pull back your hair and take your make-up off. We just put the masks on, so you can still catch up."

"Look what I brought for us," Annie said with a devilish laugh. "All the makings for a big juicy Thermos of Touch & Goes to get us in the party mood. This should get us to Keokuk in fine order."

"Annie, you've got to be kidding," Jayne said as Annie unveiled the beer and gin. "I spend half of my time warning people about the dangers of drinking and driving. You're nuts."

"Then *you* drive and *we'll* drink," Annie said as if it were the perfect compromise.

"Wow, Touch & Goes," Mebo sighed. "That really takes me back."

Annie gathered her hair into a ponytail and reached for a tissue to wipe off her make-up. "I haven't been to Keokuk, Iowa, since I was eighteen years old. Is The Dock still there?"

The other two women shrugged.

"Ain't nothing wrong that The Dock can't cure,"

sang Mebo.

The facial mask was supposed to be left on for fifteen minutes and The Three spent it reminiscing, but avoiding any talk about Sarah. As the masks dried, it became harder for them to talk and they fell into a comfortable silence while they listened to Jayne's old Bob Dylan album.

Annie was leaning back against Jayne's bed with her eyes closed, listening to the lyrics and feeling more mellow than she had in months.

"She makes love just like a woman, But she breaks just like a little girl …" Dylan's whining voice filled her head.

I broke just like a little girl.

Annie's eyes shot open, and she looked at Jayne and Mebo to see if they heard it too, but their eyes were closed, and they looked totally at peace. She got up and went into Jayne's bathroom to wash off the blue, crackled face. It felt good to let the warm water wash the mask away, and she scrubbed her face harder than was necessary. She wished Sarah's voice would disappear down the drain with the blue water.

"We really have to talk about all this tonight," Annie said into the mirror.

"Annie, what are you doing in there?" Jayne called from the other room. "It's not time yet."

"No, Jayne, I think maybe it's *past* time," she replied as she came back into the bedroom and popped the top off a warm beer.

"Okay," Mebo sounded happy and young again. "What's the next step to this *faaaabulous* makeover?"

"Make-up and hair and then we're outta here," Jayne sang on her way to the bathroom to wash off her mask.

Minutes later, as Jayne put hot rollers in Mebo's hair, Annie put on her make-up and said, "Remember how, when Sarah moved here, she just sort of latched on to us?"

The other two stopped what they were doing and looked at Annie somberly.

Annie didn't wait for a response, "She used to ask me all sorts of questions about The Three—what we did, when we met … I remember one time when I gave her a ride home after choir practice our junior year, she interrogated me about Happy Mountain."

"How'd she know about Happy Mountain?" Mebo was indignant.

"Well, I don't know. How did anybody know about it? She didn't know where it was or anything, just that it existed and that it was special to us." Annie continued, "I felt violated. I didn't want her to have anything to do with Happy Mountain."

"Yeah, that's right," Mebo recalled. "She tried so hard to be one of us. She didn't understand that The Three couldn't have four members." Mebo continued with her memories. "Good ol' Happy Mountain. We spent a lot of time there, didn't we? I had my first drink there."

"Touch & Goes!" they chimed in unison.

"As I recall, you blew your lunch that night, Meebs," Jayne chastised. "And your breakfast and your dinner. I don't recall you having very much fun that night. I was so mad at Bob for bringing that Thermos."

"Yes, *Mother*," Annie rolled her eyes. "You could be such a party-pooper, Jayne. You and Peter Perfect didn't imbibe much—not like the rest of us anyway. And the only reason I kept taking Greg back to Happy Mountain was because he was such a party animal. That's really about all he was good for. A fun way to pass through the high school years. One of us had to keep our life in perspective while the two of you were so madly in love."

The conversation paused as Mebo washed her face.

"I can't believe you left all these great albums at your mom's, Jayne." Annie was flipping through a stack of records. She pulled out Carole King's *Tapestry*, blew a dust goober off the needle, and put the disc on Jayne's old stereo.

> *My life has been a tapestry*
> *Of rich and royal hue,*
> *An everlasting vision*
> *With an ever changing view.*

Annie sang along with the music, "Ain't that the truth." She continued to listen to the music, and the memories of Happy Mountain became almost real enough for her to touch.

Happy Mountain was about two acres of woods on Mebo's Uncle Mike's farm. It was an island of trees in an ocean of cornfields. The Three had found it one spring day when they were looking for woods to take pictures for a freshman media class project. They dubbed it Happy Mountain and begged their parents to let them camp out there on the weekend. They joked about officially moving the Main Office out there, since they had outgrown the cherry trees.

For a year they kept the location secret from everyone but their parents, and of course, Mebo's uncle. It was a big move when they decided to invite their boyfriends there for a wiener roast when they were sophomores and they swore the boys to secrecy. The Three had Happy Mountain to themselves until Bob brought the Thermos of Touch & Goes, and then the atmosphere at the secret place was changed forever. They made a pact that none of them would ever go to the mountain without the others. Annie thought with satisfaction that was one promise they had all kept.

Jayne took the rollers out of Mebo's hair and finished her make-up. "Hum, I think just a little green eye shadow," Jayne said thoughtfully. "You used to wear a green eye shadow all the time." She dabbed a hint of green onto Mebo's eye lids and stood back to admire her work. "Oh, Mary Elizabeth Briget O'Cullin," Jayne cooed, "you're beautiful!"

Mebo stood and looked at her reflection in the full-length mirror on the back of the closet door. She touched her hair cautiously.

Annie stood behind her, looking over Mebo's shoulder. "You look like you did twenty years ago. You're beautiful," Annie said earnestly.

Tears began to well in Mebo's eyes.

With a Little
Help from
My Friends

THE BEATLES

Oh, I get by
With a little help from my friends.
Gonna try
With a little help from my friends.

Mebo couldn't stop staring at her reflection in Jayne's mirror, and tears started to well up in her sparkling green eyes.

"Oh, Meebs," Jayne said soothingly, "are you getting all teary on us?"

"No, stop," cried Annie, "You'll wreck your make-up!"

Mebo fought the tears, "Oh you guys, what happened to us?" The mood in the room suddenly changed. "We were so close. We shared everything. Remember when we first met when we were just little kids, and all the years in the Main Office in Jayne's back yard? There wasn't anything we didn't know about each other. I really felt closer to The Three than I did to my own family. Even when we all started dating, there was still a bond between us that mere boys could never break."

"It really was something else how close we were," Jayne remarked. "We'll probably never find such a strong relationship again. There's something about friendships begun in childhood. They're more intense than anything that comes later."

"This weekend is like we never grew up. It doesn't really feel like we've just been keeping in touch through Christmas cards and short visits every few years," Mebo added. "I always felt that when you two left to go seek your fortunes, I was left behind with some bad memories. It never really seemed the same between us after Sarah's disappearance, and I never understood why. She was never a part of us, but still she was able to nearly shatter what we had."

"I never knew you felt abandoned, Meebs," Annie combed her hair in front of the mirror at the dressing table. "After we were all questioned about Sarah's disappearance, I always felt like maybe you and Jayne blamed me."

"Why would we blame *you*, Annie?" Jayne asked gently. "You didn't have anything to do with Sarah's problems."

"Ehhh ..." Annie winced, staring at her reflection in the mirror, "I might have. I was pretty awful to her. And there must be some reason why I keep hearing her voice."

Mebo felt as if she were suffocating. She had to get out of the room, away from thinking about Sarah. "I'd better call home and see if the place is still standing." Mebo looked at her watch. "It's five thirty and Bob's been on his own with the kids all day. He's going to be fit to be tied."

She went to the phone in the family room and as she dialed her number the full impact of what she'd done hit her. She had yelled at Bob and then left him with the kids for a whole day. Her hands shook and she had to redial. The shaking spread up her arms and throughout her body. Before the phone started to ring, she slammed the receiver back on its cradle. "Okay," she mumbled to herself, "he's not your father. You're a grown-up now."

She forced herself to take several deep breaths as she imagined what Annie would say if she were in this situation. She dialed her number again, this time buoyed by the self-assurance she had borrowed from Annie.

"Hello," Bella answered the phone.

"Hi, Honey," Mebo sounded as if nothing was out of the ordinary.

"Hi, Mom," Bella's voice was cheerful. "Are you guys having fun?"

"Except for the funeral we're having a great time. Is your dad at home?"

"Yeah, just a minute," Bella called her father and laid the receiver on the table.

Mebo heard Bella tell him who it was.

"Hi, Brig," Bob's voice was almost pleasant.

"Hi," she was trying hard to keep her voice from shaking. "Is everything all right?"

"Yeah, we're fine. When do you think you'll be home?"

Mebo was confused by his nonchalance. "I'll probably be late. We're planning on going to Keokuk and we've got a lot to talk about."

Bob was silent for a second, "Well, be careful."

She couldn't imagine why he wasn't yelling at her. He sounded so neutral. "Well, I'll see you," she said and hung up. She stood for a while, staring at the phone, wondering what had just happened.

Annie appeared in the door of the family room with a tray of Touch & Goes.

"Just what the doctor ordered," Annie sang as she entered the room. "So, what did Bob say?" Annie took a sip from one of the glasses and made a face at it.

"He said, 'Be careful,'" Mebo picked up a glass and smelled its contents.

"That's all?" Annie asked incredulously.

"That's all." Mebo took a deep draught from the glass. "I made believe I had your strength. I think I blew him away."

"My strength?" Annie shrugged. "Why not? We'd better get this Touch & Go to Jayne before it eats through the glass."

Giggling, the women went to find their friend.

I Feel the Earth Move

CAROLE KING

Oh, darlin', when you're near me,
And you tenderly call my name,
I know that my emotions,
Are something I just can't tame.

Jayne came downstairs and met Annie and Mebo on their way up. They were both sipping on the T&Gs Annie had mixed.

"Here, Jayne," Annie said between sips, "This TaG's for you."

"I'll pass, Annie," Jayne felt like the killjoy they accused her of being. "I'm going to drive, remember? You guys go ahead, and when we get back here, I'll have a few and catch up with you." She handed her glass to Annie, who eventually stopped protesting and took it. Then Jayne went into the kitchen and opened a Diet Coke.

"Well, Meebs, how's it going at home?" Jayne asked when she came back into the room.

"They're all just fine, Bob says. I guess they can get along without me." Mebo waved her empty glass at Annie, who handed her Jayne's orphaned drink.

"If you two are going to start drinking that paint thinner, we better get some food into you," Jayne shook her head. "Do you want to just grab something at Keokuk?" she asked them.

"What was the name of that little dive in Sigley that made those great breaded tenderloin sandwiches and those to-die-for fries?" Annie's face brightened.

"Oh, Ramsey's," Mebo answered matter-of-factly. "Yeah, it's still there."

"We've *got* to go there. We'll hit it on the way to Keokuk. Can we huh? Please, please?" Annie was jumping up and down like a little kid.

"Do you think we'll be overdressed? Our jeans don't have any holes in them," Jayne said wryly.

The Three laughed. Mebo set down her drink and boogied around the room. Her silliness was contagious, and soon The Three were singing, "We're off to eat at Ramsey's!"

Jayne found some plastic cups and a big picnic Thermos in her mom's cabinets, and they dumped in the beer, gin and Squirt. Annie tasted the concoction and pronounced it ready to travel. In spite of her friends' protests, Jayne locked the Thermos in the trunk of her car.

Jayne turned on her CD player and The Moody Blues were singing, "Isn't Life Strange?" Annie leaned over and turned up the volume. She turned and sang to Mebo who was giggling and already feeling no pain.

Whenever Mebo didn't know the words, she made them up, usually singing something about eating tenderloins at Ramsey's. "Please pass the mustard to pour on this loin."

"You guys!" Jayne yelled, "I can't even hear myself think!" She turned down the volume.

Annie sat back down in her seat and pretended to pout. "You're no fun, Jayney," she said in a child's voice.

Jayne flipped Annie the bird, and they all laughed loudly.

"I know why she's acting like that," Mebo teased. "We're going to Sigley and she's thinking about Peter Perfect."

"Oh, Peter," Annie joined, in, "Your peter's sooo perrrfect."

"You two are hopeless, Jayne sighed. Then in a slightly more serious mood she added, "You know, I always think about driving by his parents' house whenever I drive through Sigley, but I never have." Jayne glanced over at Annie and gave her a wicked little laugh and the mood became lighter again.

They were just pulling into Sigley. Jayne drove past Ramsey's and turned on the street where Peter's parents lived. "We'll just drive by fast and lay on the horn for old time's sake," Jayne was giggling. She had just hit the horn when she noticed a red LaBaron convertible with Missouri license plates parked in the drive. Without thinking she stepped on the brakes.

Peter and a little boy were playing basketball on the

court that Peter's father put in for him on the side of the garage. Her eyes met Peter's a split second before she stepped on the accelerator and sped away. The whole episode lasted a few seconds, but to Jayne it seemed like hours, and it left her shaking.

"That was him. *God*, I don't believe it. He hasn't changed a bit! I hope he didn't realize it was me, making a complete fool of myself. Oh, shit, why did I drive by there?" The words came in a flood and Jayne trembled all the way to Ramsey's.

"Hell, Jayne, chill out." Annie was tickled by the whole event. "I'm sure he didn't know it was you, and anyway, it was great seeing him again wasn't it? Kind of gets the ol' heart pumping, huh?"

"He really did look good, Jayne," Mebo said as the car came to a stop in front of Ramsey's. From the back seat she squeezed Annie's shoulder in a sign of conspiracy.

Ramsey's looked the same as always. The floor was still well-worn, speckled gray linoleum. Formica and chrome tables were scattered throughout the large room. Cracks in the red, vinyl chair seats revealed tufts of yellowed foam stuffing. Greasy, plastic red roses adorned each table. All six patrons turned to look at The Three as they entered and found the best table by the window.

A plump, pimply girl who looked to be about sixteen appeared at their table, holding a pencil in one hand and a light green order pad in the other. She smiled, brushed her stringy hair out of her face, and popped her gum while she waited for them to tell her what they wanted. The menu was scrawled on a dusty chalkboard over the counter.

Jayne looked at her friends and raised her eyebrows in a question, then turned back to the waitress and said, "We want three tenderloin baskets and three iced teas." Seeing Peter had thrown off her center of gravity and Jayne had to force herself to behave normally.

The waitress scribbled on her pad, nodded, and walked back to the kitchen.

"Talkative little gal, isn't she?" Jayne whispered to her friends.

"You know who that is?" Mebo was quickly becoming their authority on local matters. "It's Greg Owen's daughter. Monica, I think her name is. You remember Greg, Annie."

"Damn, she could have been mine if I would have played my cards right," Annie shot them a wicked smile.

The other two started laughing. "You are *really* bad, Annie!" Mebo scolded.

The laughter took control of Annie first, then the other two. The table shook. Annie leaned across the table, "I'm going to pee my pants again." She mouthed the words silently.

Mebo scooted forward until her face was inches away from Annie's and whispered, "When you gotta go, you gotta go."

Annie excused herself. The baskets arrived before she came back. Jayne and Mebo were already pouring catsup on the paper that lined the baskets when she walked back to the table.

"That was a cultural experience," Annie said ironically. She started to say something else when she looked out the window behind Jayne and smiled broadly. "I think the fun is starting," she said as she sat down.

Peter walked in and right up to their table. Jayne froze when he sat down, across from her. "I thought that was The Three," he smiled with his whole face. "What brings you to Sigley?"

"We came for the best damn tenderloins in the country," Annie said with her mouth full.

"We've been having Touch & Goes," Mebo whispered it as if it were a secret. She'd already finished half of her tenderloin.

"Touch & Goes?" Peter broke into a new smile, one of reminiscence. "I never would have guessed you'd been drinking."

His blue eyes sparkled when they met Jayne's. She felt her heart pounding in her throat.

"I'm driving." It was all she could think to say.

"My same old cautious Jayne," Peter said without taking his eyes off her. His smile seared Jayne's soul. Even though she hadn't heard his voice for twenty years, it was as familiar to her as her own. She knew that if she spoke she would open that part of her that belonged to him, and she would be defenseless. The smell of him reanimated long dormant memories.

Annie came to her rescue, "So what brings *you* to Sigley, Peter?"

"I brought my son, Seth, to visit his grandparents," Peter explained. "I have him for a month every summer. This year I'm taking the whole month off and we're doing fun things. We're going to go to Six Flags next week, but I think Seth would rather stay in Sigley. He thinks it's the center of the Universe."

Peter's sandy hair was thinning slightly. He looked like he worked out regularly and moved with the same confidence he had so many years ago on the basketball court. There wasn't a hint of a spare tire under his blue polo shirt.

Jayne tried to eat a French fry, but her mouth was too dry, so she took a sip of her iced tea. Her trembling rattled the ice and she hoped he didn't notice. "You look great, Peter," Jayne found the words somewhere. She was trying hard not to act like the teenager she felt.

"Thank you," Peter smiled again.

Jayne began to feel her defenses melt away.

"You look better than ever," he continued. "What are you doing now?"

"I'm a therapist. I have a practice in Des Moines." Her words sounded foolish to her. There was so much more she wanted to say. In the world between sleeping and waking she had practiced saying so much more for so many years.

"A therapist?" Peter leaned forward, and Jayne noticed the way his powerful shoulders strained against his shirt. "Like a physical therapist?"

"Like a psychologist-type therapist," Jayne couldn't think of anything to say.

The question shouted in her head, "Where are the words?"

"So is it Dr. Jayne now?"

"The only time I use Dr. is when I'm making reservations," she replied.

"That fits," Peter said thoughtfully. "I'll bet you're a good therapist. Married?"

"Divorced," Jayne mumbled.

She thought she saw approval dance across his face.

"So, are you three out for a hot night on the town?" he asked them.

"We're going to Keokuk," Mebo giggled.

Jayne had forgotten that Mebo and Annie were still there. She felt her face redden as she saw the laughter in their eyes.

"And we'd better get going," Mebo continued.

When Mebo and Annie pushed away from the table, Peter reached out and touched Jayne's hand sending a lightning bolt through her body. She tried unsuccessfully to rise.

"Can I have a card from this practice in Des Moines?" Peter asked.

Jayne tore herself away from the grip his smile had on her and fished in her purse for one of her business cards, found one, and handed it to him.

He took it and produced one of his cards for her. She realized, as she took it, that she hadn't even asked him what he did. She slipped it in her purse without reading it.

"It was really nice seeing you all again," he smiled, this time at Mebo and Annie.

"Small world, isn't it?" Annie was grinning.

Peter started to walk out of the diner, then he stopped and turned back to The Three. "Hey, do you guys remember that Simpson girl who disappeared?"

"Sarah," Annie breathed.

All three of them froze where they stood.

"Yeah, Sarah," Peter echoed. "Her little brother just joined our firm." He was unaware of the women's reactions. "It really *is* a small world."

Bridge over Troubled Water

SIMON & GARFUNKEL

If you need a friend,
I'm sailing right behind.

When they got to the car, Annie took the keys out of Jayne's hand. "I'll drive," she said to Jayne. "I only had two drinks and those greasy fries took care of that. Besides, you're shaking too much to drive."

Jayne shrugged her agreement and got in on the passenger side.

"Oh sure," Mebo pretended to pout. "Stick me in the back again."

"Three quarters of a tank of gas, a trunk full of Touch & Goes, and five miles from Keokuk," Annie said in a low voice. "It's light out and we aren't wearing sunglasses. Hit it!"

When they had left Sigley, Annie looked over at Jayne. "You were really smooth back there, by the way," she teased.

Mebo burst out laughing, "I've never seen you so tongue-tied, Jayne."

"Yeah, and she forgot all about her poor friends,"

added Annie. "She was too interested in Peter's tender loins."

"Oh Gawd, Annie!" Mebo began laughing hard. She pounded the seat trying to catch her breath and snorted, "Tender loins ..."

"Okay, okay," Jayne knew she was going to be ribbed about the way she went goo-goo over Peter. "Go on. Get it out of your systems. I just can't believe I'd run into him *now*. It isn't as if we didn't have enough to figure out this weekend. We have got to figure this *Sarah thing* out before the night is over." Jayne beat her fists against the dash.

"But not right now," Annie decided for the group. The Three endured a long few seconds of silence.

Mebo broke the dark mood. "Peter's buns were as cute as ever."

"How do you know how cute his buns were, are ... ever were," Jayne sputtered, obviously still shaken.

"What about you, Annie," Mebo hung over the back of their seat until her head was nearly even with theirs. "Tell me about your love life. Your current love life, that is."

"I work real hard at not having one," Annie replied.

"Come on, Annie, you couldn't have changed that much. There's got to be someone in your life," Mebo badgered.

"Okay, okay, I'll tell you," Annie gave in, "but it's not a pretty picture."

Annie described Patrick. She told them about his

receding hairline, his paunch, and his love of cooking. She told them he was an orthodontist from Manhattan and had been married for twelve years and divorced for two. She told them that he sent her flowers every Monday, because he knew that she hated Mondays.

"Gosh, Annie, he sounds perfect," Mebo gushed. "But what about … you know … his throbbing manhood?"

"Oh my God, Mebo," said Jayne while Mebo giggled.

Annie replied in serious conspiratorial tone, "I have two words to say about that." The car was silent for two seconds as the women glanced from friend to friend, a bawdy laugh lying just below the surface.

"Bull Winkle," pronounced Annie.

"Yah!" Mebo clapped and cheered, and Jayne laughed so hard no sound came out for a while.

"Glad to hear you haven't lost your appreciation for a good throbbing manhood," Jayne was finally able to say.

"Bulging member," squeaked Mebo. "Luv cannon," added Annie.

"Enough, enough," Jayne was trying to catch her breath.

"Pulsing projectile, sex saber, randy rod," Annie clicked the names off in a dry business-like fashion.

"Um … um … Mr. Happy!" Mebo shouted proudly.

All semblance of Annie's calm demeanor was blown away and she pulled the car safely to the side of the highway and doubled over in laughter.

"Seriously," said Jayne when they'd regained some composure, "why haven't you married him?"

"That's what he wants to know," said Annie flatly and pulled the car back onto the highway. "I get all psyched and I think I can do it and then I just freak. Sometimes I think he's just too ... too," Annie stumbled, "too *good*." She added dryly, "Sarah keeps telling me that, too."

A hush fell over the car.

"Annie, nobody could be too good for you," Jayne said, pushing the picture of Sarah out of their minds. "Nobody could be too good for one of The Three."

"Amen to that," added Mebo.

"Okay, you guys," Annie laughed and shook her head, "I have a therapist of my own." She had been working on self-esteem in therapy for years. Outwardly, she was a tough publisher and a shrewd business woman, but when it came to Patrick it was a different story. It was impossible for her to believe that someone as wonderful as Patrick could love her. But as many times as she'd tested him, he'd passed with flying colors. It was as if he understood her better than she understood herself. He knew all the rotten stuff about her and he loved her anyway. He knew all the rotten stuff, with one big exception.

Annie paused while deciding whether or not to tell her friends about her most current inner conflict. "Oh, what the hell, I might as well tell you the whole story," she took a deep breath and plunged in.

"A couple of months ago a nineteen year-old boy came to work in the mail room," she paused for a second. It was hard to muster enough breath to continue.

"This kid is *so* beautiful—incredible eyes. He makes me feel eighteen. It seems like I've known him for a long time. Anyway, I know it's a stupid thing to do, but I can't help it. I've been majorly boinking him since the second day he was there. I'm probably sabotaging my relationship with Patrick. If he ever found out, it would be all over. *Why do I do this?* I think I really love Patrick, but love doesn't enter into this thing with the boy."

"Sounds to me like you know what you need to do," Jayne said gently.

Explaining it all to Mebo and Jayne had made her understand it herself. Annie began to see this was one of the things that made her relationship with these women so special. They loved her just the way she was. Annie felt good.

"Maybe I *will* marry Patrick," she smiled.

"That a girl," Mebo piped in. "No guts, no glory, Mrs. Bull Winkle. Are we almost there? I've got to tinkle."

"Perfect timing, Meebs, we're just about to go over the bridge. You'll have to hold it 'til we ..." Annie dropped her thought mid-sentence. "The gas station just on the other side. Is it still there?" She asked.

"Yeah," Mebo answered, "but hurry on across. I have weak kidneys."

The car pulled up to the toll booth on the Iowa side

of the Mississippi River. Annie rolled the window down and read the sign, "Twenty-five cents? Haven't they paid for this bridge by now?"

As Annie handed the toll man two quarters, she said, "This takes care of the next car to come along. Tell them it's compliments of *The Three*."

"Annie, you're crazy," Jayne laughed.

"Oh no, you guys, don't make me laugh. I'm going to pee," Mebo was holding her sides.

"You're in luck, Mary Elizabeth, pit stop ahead," Annie announced. She pulled the car around to the side of the gas station.

Mebo jumped out of the back seat and ran up to the ladies' room door and found it locked. She held her stomach and made faces toward the car as she ran around to the front to get the key from the attendant. The car shook again with laughter.

Mebo was back in a few minutes and slid into the back seat. "Guys, I was thinking," Mebo said, seriously, "and I wanted to get you something to celebrate the men of your dreams. So I got you these."

With that she thrust a condom under each of their noses and said, "Look, no pin holes."

The car was up for grabs. Jayne laughed so hard, she snorted. Annie couldn't catch her breath and her face looked purple under the florescent lights of the gas station. The car bounced as a result of Mebo pounding the back seat. The gas station attendant, who only minutes before looked like one of the walking dead, left his post behind the counter to peek out the door at them.

"Do you believe we used to sneak into the men's room at Conoco, break into the machine and put pin holes in the rubbers?" Annie gasped.

Jayne wiped the tears off her cheeks. "I wonder how many shot gun marriages we were responsible for?"

The thought sobered Annie, and her face returned to its normal color.

"If I ever thought my girls did anything like that," Mebo sat up in her seat, "I'd break their knees."

Annie looked at Jayne, "You've got mascara all over your face. You better fix it before we get to The Dock."

(Sittin' on) the Dock of the Bay

OTIS REDDING

I'm just sittin' on the dock of the bay,
wasting time.

The parking lot at The Dock was packed. Annie had to park in the corner farthest from the street and the entrance. The car heaved and bounced its way through the potholes.

"You'd think we would have given this place enough business to have the parking lot paved," Mebo was bouncing in the back seat. "Get your IDs ready."

"Yeah, right!" Annie feigned disgust, "Somehow, I don't think we're going to be carded this time."

"How many times did we come to this bar?" Jayne mused. "I used to drink my Diet Coke while you two got blotto, then I'd drive you home, safe and sound."

"Sister Jayne", Mebo laughed. "I'm glad the drinking age isn't still eighteen in Iowa. If they don't check IDs any more carefully than they used to when we were in high school, I think I'd better start keeping Betsy and Bella on a short leash."

"This is going to be great," Annie squealed, rubbing

her hands together in anticipation. "We're sure to see somebody we know in here."

"The band must be on break," Mebo said as they approached the entrance. "I can't hear any music."

The burley bouncer greeted them with a look of surprised amusement as they entered the dimly lit bar.

"Boy, has this place changed!" Mebo looked around and led her friends to a table in the corner.

A candle twinkled under an amber glass cover in the middle of the table. As their eyes adjusted to the darkness, a slim, effeminate young man in an apron appeared at the side of the table and asked them what he could do for them.

Mebo and Annie ordered Miller Lites and Jayne ordered her usual Diet Coke.

"I can't believe this place," exclaimed Mebo. "It's clean and everything." Annie and Jayne smiled at each other as their friend continued. "It used to be so loud in here you had to yell to be heard."

The waiter brought their drinks and Mebo took a long draught from hers. She looked disappointed, "I really wanted to dance."

Annie started to laugh out loud and Jayne kicked her under the table.

"What's with you two?" asked Mebo.

"You're right, Meebs," Annie snickered. "This place has *really* changed."

"Or maybe it was always a quiet little bar and just pretended to be a rowdy hole-in-the-wall," Jayne giggled. "Let's just finish this one and get out of here."

Annie chugged her beer. "I'm ready," she said.

"God, Annie," Mebo laughed. "Oh, what the hell." She chugged her beer, too.

Jayne didn't bother finishing her Coke.

As they stood up from their table, Mebo noticed a tall, great-looking man who had just come in. He acted as if he were looking for someone. He spotted the subject of his search, smiled, then walked over to a table just in front of Mebo. He leaned down and kissed the man who was waiting for him.

Annie and Jayne watched Mebo and anticipated her reaction. Annie grabbed their stunned buddy's left arm as Jayne grabbed her right arm and they nearly carried her from the bar before she could do any more than gasp.

"Our friend had a little too much to drink," Jayne apologized to the bouncer as they bundled her off to the car.

Once inside the car, Jayne and Annie started laughing uncontrollably again.

"Mebo, I can't believe you," Annie blurted out.

"But, Annie," Mebo still looked as if she just saw aliens land in the middle of the Dodge Square. "Those men were *kissing*—full on the mouth!"

"Yes, Mary Elizabeth Briget," Jayne felt as if she were explaining algebra to her. "The Dock is now a gay bar."

"Oh, my God," Mebo sounded alarmed. "Do you

think the beer was alright?"

Annie was sore from laughing and from trying to keep from laughing. "I'm opening the trunk," she said. "You can drive, Jayne."

Spinning Wheel

BLOOD, SWEAT & TEARS

Talking about your troubles,
It's a crying sin,
Ride a painted pony,
Let the spinning wheel spin.

Annie opened the trunk and quickly poured two glasses from the big Thermos. She and Mebo drank them while Jayne tried to explain the difference between gays and serial murderers.

They decided to forego any more bar-hopping and head to Happy Mountain and get to the task at hand. The trip home was filled with more laughter, punctuated with one stop. On a dark country road three miles outside of Dodge, at 9:37 p.m., three 38 year-old women relieved themselves in the ditch.

"I see your 3s," shouted Mebo to her friends as they pulled down their pants, revealing the matching tattoos they got twenty years ago on their Last Fling.

"I see your 3," the two shouted back.

When they got to Dodge, Jayne drove to the Square where they took their place in the regular Saturday night parade. It was a Dodge phenomenon that on Saturday nights the teenagers drove their cars around and around the Square, three deep, at 5 miles per hour.

"I wondered if they still did this," Jayne shook her head in disbelief.

"Kids have been driving around the Square as long as they've been making cars, I think," Mebo added with some pride. "Bob and my record is 50 times around in one night. Sort of says something about going nowhere, doesn't it," Mebo sounded sad.

Maybe it was the rediscovered confidence that came from being part of The Three or maybe it was the beer and the Touch & Goes, something had given voice to the ideas that had been churning inside of Mebo for the past few years. "I don't know what happened to us. In some ways it doesn't seem that long ago that he was this big football hero and I was a skinny little cheerleader. And you were right, Jayne, all I wanted was to marry Bob and live happily ever after," Mebo was staring out the window and seeing her life.

"So I wasn't very upset at all when I got pregnant. I knew Bob would marry me. I don't think anybody was surprised. We'd only been married a month when I lost the baby," her voice quivered. Then for a moment, the occupants of the car listened to the muffled sounds of the radio and voices of the other paraders.

"I know you'll probably think this is weird, since I have five kids now, but sometimes I still wake up at night crying about that baby I lost." A hollow silence again filled the car as it continued on its slow circuit. "Then I didn't get pregnant again for three years, and we were really trying. I started feeling like I couldn't do anything right." Mebo's tongue was loosened now and her friends let her ramble.

"I don't know. When the twins were born, I was so busy that I didn't have time to think about how I felt about Bob. Then Brad came along and I started feeling like somebody's mother or somebody's wife all the time. Then before I knew it, I didn't have a clue who I was, but I was sure I didn't like me very much. I always thought that everything would be all right once we built our house. I guess it seems silly to pin so much on a house, but we did. We planned and planned and saved every penny for that house."

Mebo looked silently out the window for a second, "Then, a year ago, it was just gone. We were going to sleep in our new house the next night. But the next night the house had disappeared. Nothing but ashes."

"Did you ever find out what caused the fire?" asked Annie.

"We know *who* caused the fire and that makes it ever more painful."

"We had a young man a few years older than the twins working with Bob. He was a really good worker and he became like one of the family. The girls were crazy about him because he treated them like little sisters. He'd been with us all summer and helped us build the house. We did almost all the work ourselves. He disappeared the night of the fire. When the fire marshal determined that it was intentionally set, our hearts sank. To think that this kid, who we all loved and who Bob treated like a son ... to think that he destroyed our dreams. Well, it was just too much. They never caught him."

Her voice was hollow now. "That's when Bob really changed toward me. He started treating me really bad. He doesn't hit me or anything, but he talks to me like I'm dirt, and that hurts worse. And then there's always Sarah," Mebo shivered. "I kept thinking I must be crazy. Even now I can't think of a better explanation."

The silence was piercing this time. Mebo began again, as much to break the silence as anything.

"I know Bob doesn't feel very good about himself, either. He had such plans. We were going to own our own farm. The house was just the beginning. He wanted to have cattle. But instead we're renting Uncle Mike's farm and just making ends meet."

"Speaking of the farm," Mebo tried to shake the heaviness of the remembrance from the car," we're going to have to go the back way to Happy Mountain, so Bob won't see the headlights."

"I've got a flashlight in the glove compartment," Jayne said, taking the opportunity to escape the Square. "Check and see if the batteries are any good."

Annie pulled a long, red flashlight from the glove compartment. She turned it on and held it under her chin so it shined up over her face, casting eerie shadows.

She turned to face Mebo and in a spooky voice sang,

"Teen Angel, can you hear me?"

The Three giggled and then fell silent again as one by one they became aware of the irony of the song.

Fire and Rain

JAMES TAYLOR

Lord knows, when the cold wind blows,
It'll turn your head around.

They parked the car on the side of the gravel road. Annie hugged the Thermos of Touch & Goes to her while Mebo led the way with the flashlight and the plastic cups.

When Jayne retrieved a blanket from the trunk of her car, Annie said, "My God, Jayne, you are so practical and organized! I'll bet you put a fresh box of baking soda in your fridge exactly every three months."

Jayne fussed with the blanket, folding it into a smaller bundle and without looking away from it, and feeling slightly guilty, said, "Well, yes … actually, I do."

Annie elbowed Mebo and they laughed at their friend.

"She probably has 'change the baking soda in fridge' written on her calendar along with 'fertilize house plants,'" Mebo giggled.

Jayne playfully shoved her friends ahead of her and the intimacy of their friendship warmed her. They walked across fifty yards of pasture and found a path into the brush and trees that made up Happy Mountain.

"I don't remember it being this overgrown," Jayne complained, trying to dislodge a tentacle of multiflora rose that had grabbed onto her jeans.

"I think we'd better just stay on this path and see where it leads," Annie suggested. She grabbed hold of Mebo who was searching the ground ahead of them with the flashlight. "Stay together."

Mebo began, "Brad and Benny spend a lot of time out here trying to trap animals. I think they made a tree house here somewhere. That's why there are paths and ..." She stopped and swept the flashlight around a clearing about twelve feet in diameter. "Ta da," she sang with an air of accomplishment. "Do you think this was our campsite?" Mebo knelt to inspect a ring of stones that marked the place where a campfire had been.

"Could be. How bizarre," Annie replied as she sat down the Thermos. "But even if it isn't, we can pretend it is. Jayne, how about if we spread the blanket here and pour some refreshments?"

"Oooh, do you think my kids have been coming to Happy Mountain?" Mebo said shivering. "That seems wrong. Like incest or something."

Annie was using the flashlight to pour Touch & Goes and hesitated at her friend's analogy.

Jayne spread the blanket by moonlight. "Oh, pour one for me," she said decidedly. "I think I have some catching up to do." She took a sip from the cup Annie handed her and made a face. "This is terrible. It's as bad as I imagined."

Annie held up her hand to Mebo, who laughed as she gave her friend a high five.

"Can we build a little fire here, Mebo?" Jayne asked as she stirred the old ashes with a stick.

"Yeah, let's find some firewood," she answered. "They won't be able to see it from the house."

The Three combed the clearing and came up with a pile of sticks big enough to start a small fire. As they all squatted around the fire site, they realized that none of them knew how to start a fire without crumpled paper for kindling. It was obvious that the sticks were too big for Annie to ignite with the matches she took from The Dock.

"I have a gas lighter in my fireplace at home," Mebo said helplessly. "Wait, what am I thinking?" She sat up with an air of determination and said, "I can do this. I wasn't a Cub Scout den mother for three years for nothing."

"Go find me some dry leaves, Jayne," Mebo ordered as she searched the ground and came up with a handful of brittle twigs and pine needles.

Jayne returned with an armful of papery brown oak leaves. The den mother chose two rocks from the ring that encircled the fire site and placed them about a foot apart in the center of the ring. She rested a stick on the two rocks, creating a bridge, then placed a handful of the collected kindling below the stick. She carefully leaned first the twigs, then bigger and bigger sticks against the bridge stick in a criss-cross pattern, forming a teepee.

Annie illuminated her old friend's work with admiration and a flashlight.

Mebo leaned back, dusted off her hands and evaluated her handiwork. "That ought to do it," she said proudly. "Annie hand me your matches."

"And pray," Jayne added.

Mebo struck a match and held it to the leaves through a gap in the pile of twigs. The leaves smoldered, then crackled, then produced a little flame. Mebo held her breath as the flames spread to the little twigs and finally became a healthy fire. The flickering light danced across Mebo's face, which was alive with pride.

"Great job, Meebs!" Annie slapped her on the back and handed her another cup of Touch & Goes.

Jayne realized that she'd emptied her cup while she watched the fire materialize. Maybe it didn't taste so bad after all. She held her empty up to Annie for a refill and thought, "One more glass and then I'm going to tell them about Sarah."

The fire drew them in and seemed to hypnotize The Three as they quietly stared into the snapping and dancing flames. They could see the stars suspended above them in the opening of the clearing, and the moon faintly lit the areas where the firelight didn't reach. Jayne felt as if she were enclosed in a glass dome that someone had shaken, setting glitter floating through the dark liquid around them. She stayed in the semi-trance state until she realized that she had to go to the bathroom.

"Which way to the little girl's room?" Jayne stood up and brushed the grass from her jeans.

"That would be just over there," Annie pointed carelessly over her shoulder. "I'll come with you."

Mebo sat by the fire and poured another Touch & Go. Just as the other two returned to the fire, they were startled by a dark shadow that suddenly flew over the fire.

"Relax." Mebo shivered as she topped off their glasses. "It's just an owl." She retrieved the flashlight from Jayne and directed the beam to a branch about twelve feet up in the oak tree. Just a minute earlier the trunk of that tree had served as the ladies room wall. The light followed the branch until it illuminated the eyes of an owl, staring back at The Three.

Mebo dragged a dead branch to the center of the clearing and put it across the flames.

The women moved closer to the fire. They knew that the conversation they had been avoiding all weekend could no longer be postponed.

"Remember our Last Fling?" Jayne asked.

The Three lapsed into memories about the last weekend they had spent together. They graduated from Dodge High on a Thursday. For months The Three had been planning the trip to Chicago that their parents gave them as a graduation present. They left on Friday morning and, full of anticipation, drove Jayne's father's Buick into the city. They stayed at the Blackstone on Michigan Avenue. The chandeliers and opulence made them drunk.

They all would start their summer jobs when they returned—Annie and Mebo at the Dairy Dream, and Jayne at the nursing home. So, they tried to pack everything they could in to their Last Fling. They saw "Annie Get Your Gun" on stage, went to the planetarium, and spent most of their graduation money eating at ethnic restaurants and shopping at downtown stores. To immortalize the Fling they had matching 3s tattooed on their rumps.

As far as Jayne was concerned, it was the perfect adventure. Until they got home.

Jayne remembered how the nightmare began, as if it happened yesterday. She had only been home for a couple of hours that Sunday night. She was exhausted from the trip and was dumping her suitcase in the laundry room when her mother answered the phone.

The questions, the suspicion, and the confusion started with that phone call from Sarah's mother. Sarah had told her parents that she was going on the Last Fling with The Three. She packed her suitcase and drove away on Friday morning, saying the four of them would drive her car to Chicago. She even called home on Saturday afternoon and reported that they were having a great time at the Blackstone and would be back Sunday night. Sarah's parents were shocked to find out that Sarah had never been with them, nor did they ever have any intentions of including her in their trip. It was the first time the girls had heard any of this.

It was many, many months later when the police finally gave up the search. They exhausted all possibilities. Sarah's abandoned car was found only a couple of blocks from the Blackstone, but it was confirmed that she never stayed there. There were absolutely no leads, and the sympathy of the people of Dodge turned from Sarah and her parents, relative newcomers to Dodge, to The Three for being questioned so relentlessly.

A year later, Sarah's father was offered a transfer to a power plant in Tennessee, and he accepted it. He moved the remainder of his family away from the questioning looks and gave up hope of ever finding Sarah.

Jayne shook the memories from her head and continued, "There's something I never told you guys," she began her confession reluctantly. "I've always known more about Sarah than I ever told anyone."

Her friends froze as if their stillness would keep Sarah away. Jayne's heart leapt to her throat.

You swore, Jayne.

Jayne clenched her fists and crushed her empty cup. "I kept the promise all these years, Sarah!" the words exploded into the night like a shot and disturbed the owl who hooted eerily. Jayne blanched and sat shaking.

Mebo and Annie shuddered with the realization that Sarah had spoken to her.

Jayne wiped her damp hands on her jeans. She rubbed her face, took a deep breath and began again. "A week or so before graduation, Sarah came to my house. She was frantic. She told me that she knew I really didn't consider her a close friend, but that I was the only one she could talk to. She swore me to secrecy and, until now, I never told a soul."

Even though the fire made a warm night even warmer, Jayne doubled over and clutched her knees to her chest in an attempt to stop the shaking. "Sarah said she had missed two periods and she knew she was pregnant."

Mebo gasped and Annie sat silently as Jayne continued, "She told me she had gotten very drunk one night and the guy she was with turned out to be an animal. He didn't take no for an answer. When she told him later that she thought she was pregnant, he laughed at her."

Jayne sighed in exasperation," She wanted me to help her. She didn't know where to go or what to do or whom to contact, but she did know that she wanted an abortion. I told her that I wanted no part of it and I couldn't help her. At the time, I didn't even think she was telling the truth. We never talked about it again."

Midnight Confessions

GRASS ROOTS

In my midnight confessions,
when I say all the things that I want to.

When Jayne told her story, Annie felt as if someone hit her in the stomach. Every inch of Annie's head was pounding. "Pregnant? *Pregnant?*" thought Annie. "*I* did this to her. My God, it's all my fault!"

Annie and Mebo sat in total silence. Jayne's story was too unbelievable to take in. Jayne was always mature and responsible. Keeping a secret like that from her parents, the police, and even The Three just didn't fit. Annie realized that everything about their relationship to Sarah was abnormal.

Mebo finally broke the silence, "Jayne, why didn't you tell us that before? How could you keep all that to yourself? You never even told the *police* after Sarah disappeared?"

Jayne stared back over the flickering flames. Her face seemed totally drained of color. "Mebo, I gave my word."

Mebo nodded, tears streaming down her face.

"I can understand why Jayne kept that to herself all these years," Annie finally spoke. "Now it's my turn to tell you what I know."

Fortified by the Touch & Goes, Annie shared her piece of the horrendous puzzle. Jayne and Mebo stared at her as fear and the fire reflected in their eyes. There was a tightening in her throat, and Annie realized that what she was about to tell them could change the way they felt about her forever.

She poured herself another drink and suggested they do the same. She wondered how many of these she had had. It wasn't enough. After taking a very deep breath, Annie began. "What I am about to tell you is something I am not at all proud of, and it may hurt you both very much. Especially you, Meebs, but I'm not going to sugar-coat this. I've lived with it long enough."

Mebo was softly crying. She wanted to tell Annie to stay silent, that she just wanted to go home, but instead she said, "Go ahead, Annie."

With her eyes squeezed shut, Annie silently said the first prayer she'd said since she was a little girl. God didn't listen to her then. She hoped He was listening this time. She really didn't want to hurt these women. In an instant she understood what eleven years of therapy had failed to teach her—she kept her friends at a distance to protect *them*, not herself. The realization changed her. The healing began even before she told the story.

"Probably a few months before Sarah came to you,

Jayne, she came to me. She phoned me after school on a Friday afternoon and said that Bob had asked her to meet him that night after he took Mebo home from the dance."

Mebo sighed, but said nothing.

"I have no idea why she called me, but I guess she wanted to confide in someone. She wanted my advice on whether she should meet him or not." She mumbled her second prayer in two decades, "God forgive me," then resumed. "I was pissed for two reasons. One, I really didn't want her to think that I was someone she could share a secret with, and two, I was jealous because I wanted to be with Bob."

Annie rose to her knees and scooted closer to Mebo. She gently touched Mebo's shoulder and her eyes stung with tears. Mebo stiffened, sure now that she didn't want to hear whatever Annie was about to say.

"I had been seeing him, Meebs, every once in a while after he took you home at night, but then he started to ignore me."

Annie waited for a response, but Mebo sat frozen, staring at the fire.

"I told Sarah to meet me in the school parking lot before the dance," Annie shivered and took a deep breath. She knew each word was an icy dagger in Mebo's heart. "She agreed and we went in my car out to the lake. All Sarah wanted from me was advice, and all I wanted was to do was get her good and drunk, which I did. She talked, I schemed, and we both drank. That poor girl was three sheets to the wind when I dropped her off again at the school."

"That's when I saw you, Meebs, out in the parking lot sitting in your car. You told me that you and Bob had a fight and he left the dance earlier and you didn't know where he was. I jumped in your car and we talked for quite a while and then I suggested we take a drive, remember? I knew where I was taking you that night. We headed out toward the lake and found the lane on the other side of old Shot Gun Noah's shack, where Bob usually took me. Sure enough, there was his van parked along the side of the road. Mebo, you were furious. We could hear his radio and you knew Bob was with someone, but you didn't know who." Annie took another deep breath and realized her face was wet with tears.

"I really accomplished a lot that night. I got Sarah drunk and I hurt you a lot. I thought I was trying to hurt Bob that night, but I don't know, Meebs. Maybe I was really trying to hurt you."

All three were staring into the fire now, afraid to look at each other.

"I have always wanted what you have," Annie clipped the words off in staccato fashion.

Mebo pulled her eyes away from the fire and tried to focus on Annie. "What *I* have?" Mebo was trying to grasp the meaning of Annie's words.

Annie spoke as if she had to drag each word up from her toes. "When I first met you, Meebs ... well you remember what my dad was like then. I'll never forget the first time you and Jayne came to my house to play and Dad was drunk and threw Mom down in the back yard right in front of us. I thought neither of you would ever want to be my friend after that. I was so ashamed."

Mebo's voice was quivering, "You don't have to talk about it, Annie."

"No, you're wrong," Annie wiped tears from her cheeks. "I *really* need to talk about it. I spent all my life trying not to talk about it. And look where that got me."

She dug a crumpled tissue from her pocket and wiped her nose. "Whenever we were at your house, I used to imagine what it would be like to live in a family like yours. Your family always ate dinner together. You played together and laughed. I remember once, when we were in third or fourth grade, when I stayed all night at your house. Mom had a black eye when I left my house. Your dad came into your room to tuck us in at night." Annie shook visibly, and she didn't seem to notice when Jayne moved next to her and put her arm around her back. "I panicked then, Mebo. Then, when he just kissed your cheek and tucked the covers around you, and left the room ..."

Annie began sobbing, and the words came out in broken gasps, "I thought ... I thought, so *this* is the way fathers are supposed to be."

A low moan came from Mebo's throat as she realized the nightmare of Annie's youth. "I knew he was mean to you, Annie, but I never knew ..." Mebo's voice trailed off.

"Then after that, whenever my dad came into my room at night, smelling like stale cigars and whiskey ... whenever he staggered over to my bed ... I just closed my eyes as tight as I could and I became you, Mebo. I imagined what it would be like to be you. To be *normal*. To be loved. To be *clean*." The sobbing took over and Annie's body shook. She threw the soggy tissue into the fire and hid her face in her hands.

All of Mebo's anger disappeared with the tissue in the fire. She moved closer to Annie until Annie was sandwiched snugly between her and Jayne. "You are safe now." Mebo produced several folded tissues from her pocket and gave them to her friend. "I never knew. And for years I've been jealous of you. I figured that you thought you were too good for me."

Annie blew her nose, "Too good for *you*, Mebo? You are the one who is good. You and Jayne are good. I've always felt like a bad person around you guys."

The Three sat in the flickering light of the fire, holding on to each other for dear life.

"I guess I believed that I was bad, so I had to prove it to everyone. I am so sorry. I'm sorry that I acted like that. I never should have hurt you, and I never should have hurt Sarah."

From a branch above them came the low hoot of the owl. The Three looked from one to the other.

"How are you feeling, Annie?" asked Jayne nervously, slipping back into the comfort of the therapist's role.

"I feel … um, I'm not sure. I think I feel good. I feel loved."

"We have always loved you, Annie," Mebo wiped her nose on her sleeve, "even when you were a real bitch."

They laughed weakly through their sniffles.

"It was my *dad* who was bad," Annie had discovered a huge truth. "It wasn't me. It wasn't me!"

"No, Sweetie," Jayne hugged her, "you are good."

"Jesus Sweet Christ!" Annie's voice was stronger now. She looked at Mebo and then at Jayne. "I put my therapist's kids through college, and I have to come to Happy Mountain with you two to get anywhere. Do you know how much money I could have saved if we would have done this twenty years ago?"

"Twenty years ago," Jayne sounded almost apologetic to remind them, "we were all spending a lot of time talking to police."

Sounds of Silence

Simon & Garfunkel

And the vision that was planted in my brain
Still remains.

"I still can't believe you both knew something about Sarah, and you didn't tell the police anything!" Mebo shook her head in disbelief. "You didn't even tell me anything."

Jayne and Annie didn't make a sound. The night had suddenly become very dark and very still. It seemed as if The Three were totally alone in the world, except for the prying eyes of the owl above them.

Mebo picked up a stick and began poking the dwindling fire.

"Come on, Annie," Jayne said, forcing her weak legs to hold her up. "We'd better find some more fuel for this fire. I think we're going to be here for a while." They grabbed the flashlight and went off in search of firewood.

Mebo found the Thermos and emptied it into her cup. The fire had burned the branch in half and she pushed both halves into the fire with the stick. She tried to decide if she was numb from exhaustion or from the Touch & Goes. She stretched her cramped legs out in front of her and felt a shiver radiate from her spine as she sensed the owl staring at her.

You can't ignore me tonight, can you?

Mebo pushed the end of her stick into the ground beside her until it snapped with a loud crack. The sound disturbed the owl, who flapped her wings silently above her.

"What was that?" Jayne directed the beam of the flashlight on Mebo.

"Sarah," Mebo's speech was slurred. Jayne carried an arm full of sticks, and Annie dragged a fat log behind her.

"She said that I couldn't ignore her tonight," Mebo shared, steadying her cup between her feet and hugging her arms. She felt like she was telling on Sarah, and it seemed to take some of Sarah's power away. Jayne put some of the small sticks on the fire and then helped Annie lift the log onto the blaze.

"She's right, you know. I can't ignore her tonight. But I sure could ignore her before she disappeared." Mebo finished the last of the Touch & Goes and threw the empty cup onto the fire. She hugged her knees to her and rocked back and forth. "I think I ignored everybody and everything back then. In high school, my whole life was Bob and cheerleading. I couldn't see past the end of my nose. You guys were my best friends, and I didn't even know what was going on with you. I didn't know how awful things were for you, Annie. I didn't even realize, Jayne, how heartbroken you were about

Peter until I saw how you looked at him this weekend. And I certainly never had any time for Sarah. She was nothing to me. She was like a little gnat, annoying, but not very important. All she wanted was to be a part of us, and I wouldn't even look at her. It was a sin of omission and I've paid for it."

Mebo stood up and paced in front of the fire. That moment the only sounds were the crackling log and snapping fire and Mebo's footsteps crunching little twigs.

The silence was shattered by the shrill screech of the owl.

The Three caught their breath, and in the same instant Mebo scooped a small rock from the ring around the fire and threw it in the direction of the owl with a force that surprised her. "If I would have had my eyes open, I would have known she was after Bob," Mebo continued. "Annie, I didn't know that *Sarah* was the one in Bob's van with him that night, but I did know that he spent time with other girls, including you. I just convinced myself that nothing was actually going on with you two."

"I'm so sorry," Annie barley whispered the words.

Mebo sat back down by the fire facing Annie and Jayne. "Annie, if you think this revelation is going to make me hate Bob, don't worry. I gave up thinking about how he acted in high school years ago. I always knew he screwed around. He never kept that a secret from me. But to think that he got Sarah pregnant! It was his fault that Sarah disappeared. I wonder if he knew."

The Three sat silently, letting it all soak in.

"God," Mebo sighed. "If Bob knew all this time that he got Sarah pregnant ..." She quickly brought her head up and stared at Jayne with a new realization. "And if she didn't get an abortion, he could have another child somewhere! Oh, my God. That must be eating him up. He might be a little rough around the edges, and I know our relationship needs a lot of work, but Bob is crazy about his kids. It would kill him to think he might have a son or daughter that he's never seen."

"But she told me she wanted to get an abortion," Jayne threw out the words as if they were a life preserver.

"No!" Mebo slapped the ground. "That would be worse. Bob would hate that. How would she have gotten one, anyway? They weren't legal then."

"Just because they weren't legal didn't mean they weren't available," Annie explained. "Lots of people got them. I think it was pretty easy to get one in a city."

"Like Chicago," Mebo said, flatly.

You Got a Friend

CAROLE KING

Close your eyes and think of me,
And soon I will be there,
To brighten up even your darkest night.

The screeching of the owl made the women jump close to each other. The bird beat its wings and oak leaves fluttered to the ground. It swooped down within four feet of the women's heads and rose again to land on a branch on the opposite side of the clearing.

Mebo's hands dug into Annie's arms. All three hearts were beating fast.

"I don't think that bird wants us here," Jayne said, wiping her sweaty palms on her jeans. "My adrenal glands are working just fine, how about yours?"

No one laughed at Jayne's attempt to relieve the anxiety that pressed down on them like a huge weight.

"Okay, okay," Annie shook some of the tension from her hands. "It's just a big bird. I have always hated birds."

The Three sat down together, close to the fire that had consumed most of the log. Mebo put the remaining sticks on the fire and stirred it. The flames grew with the new sustenance.

"We need to face the fact that we'll probably never know what Sarah did," Jayne said.

Annie sighed in agreement.

Jayne continued, "She may be dead. Maybe she had an abortion, maybe she didn't. But whatever she did, she did it without us. It wasn't our fault. It's no wonder that we've all been haunted by guilt all these years, but it's over now." She was trying to convince herself.

They sat quietly for a moment, letting the crackling fire burn the guilt and the hurt from them.

"We all need to let Sarah go," Jayne said it to herself as much as to her friends. "It's ironic that Sarah tried so hard to be one of us—probably because she wanted to share our closeness. And she was what caused us to drift apart."

Annie leaned forward and sprinkled a handful of little twigs and leaves onto the fire. "But in the end, nothing could break up ..." She paused and looked expectantly back and forth between Jayne and Mebo.

"The Three," they all said in unison.

None of them noticed when the owl quietly flew away.

Jayne held her hand out in front of her. Annie covered Jayne's hand with her own. Mebo followed suit and added her hand. "All for one and one for all," giggled Jayne.

Mebo smiled meekly and stood up, rubbing her seat, "I am bushed! All this soul searching wore me out. I'm not used to it." Her laugh got stronger. "Is this what you do for a living, Jayne? I don't know how you stand it!"

Jayne stood yawning and brushed the leaves off her jeans, "I think that paint thinner we've been drinking has something to do with how tired we are." She held her watch so that the fire lit it enough to read. "Then again, it's 3:00 in the morning, and none of us has slept much all weekend. We're not kids anymore, you know."

"No kidding," Annie was touching her toes, trying to work some of the kinks out of her muscles. "I feel like Julian Van Pelt looks."

Mebo leaned toward Annie and sniffed, "You smell like him, too."

"So, Mebo," Jayne yawned again, "are you as good at putting out campfires as you are at building them?"

"This fire is on its last legs anyway." Mebo studied the flames and reflected on her extensive knowledge of fires. She began kicking dirt on to the flame. She found another long stick and used it to push ashes from around the firepit onto the embers. The small flames sputtered and died as Jayne gathered the blanket.

"This soldier died for a good cause," Annie said with mock solemnness as she picked up the empty Thermos. The Three made their way back to the car. They stepped over the ditch onto the gravel and turned back toward the woods.

"Well, I guess this is good-bye to Happy Mountain,"

said Annie sentimentally, "until the Second Annual Main Office Reunion."

United We Stand

BROTHERHOOD OF MAN

For united we stand, divided we fall,
And if our backs should ever be against the wall,
We'll be together.

"Wait a minute," Jayne threw out the words before she had a chance to change her mind, "as long as we're bearing souls, here—"

"Oh, please, no," Mebo sounded exasperated. "I don't think I can take any more tonight."

"No, no," Jayne assured them, "it's nothing like that. It has nothing to do with Sarah. It has nothing to do with you two either. It's just that I want to get something off my chest."

"Oh, well, what the hell," Annie closed the door as they climbed into the car. "Fire away! Whatever it is, we can take it."

Jayne began with some trepidation. "Well, both of you know that I left my practice in Minneapolis two years ago, right?" She didn't wait for an answer. "What I didn't tell you was that I really didn't have a choice in the matter."

Her friends waited patiently in the darkness.

"The patient was a seventeen year old boy. I had

been seeing him for about six months. He was de-pressed, but had been doing really well," she stumbled. "At least I thought he was doing well."

"I've been over it and over it a million times and it still doesn't make any sense."

"Jayne," Annie asked gently as she reached out to touch her friend, "what happened?"

Jayne paused a second and took a deep breath, "He accused me of seducing him. He described in great de-tail how we'd been having sex for the past six months."

"What!" Mebo shrieked. "What kind of nut was this guy?"

"Obviously more troubled than I imagined," Jayne shook her head. "I should have paid more attention to my own feelings. I became too personally involved with him, and that was wrong. I began treating him more like a son. But I *swear to God*, I did nothing to lead him on, let alone sleep with him."

"Of course you didn't," Annie said. "I'm horny enough to sleep with the mail room kid, but you? Of course you didn't!"

"I had to go before the Board of Review, and even though I was cleared of charges, too many people couldn't get past the suspicion. There was just enough publicity to ruin my career in Minneapolis. I was lucky not to lose my license." The story left a bad taste in her mouth.

Mebo whispered, "That's weird!"

"It's more than weird," Jayne replied.

Dust in the Wind

All we are is dust in the wind

Annie didn't wake Jayne when she rose Sunday morning at 8:00. Mrs. Lipton had already left for church. Annie found a pad of paper and a pen on the desk in the family room and left a note.

Dear Jayne,

Thanks for everything. For letting me stay here and for coming back to give me moral support this weekend. I know we said our good-byes last night. We'll stay in touch now that everything is worked out among The Three. Thanks for making me see that being a part of The Three is enough to get me through almost anything. Hug your mom for me. I'll call you this week.

Love, Annie

She picked up her suitcase and with her tote strap over her shoulder went out to her car. She loaded the

luggage into the trunk and stood for a minute, looking out over Jayne's back yard. She opened the door
of the car, then paused and closed the door again. She
ran out to the cherry trees, picked a few cherries and
popped them in her mouth. She smiled and lovingly
stroked a branch of the center tree before she walked
back to her car.

When she got to her house, her mother stood in the
kitchen in a faded, plaid flannel robe making coffee.
She was humming a tune as she greeted her daughter
with a smile and a little hug. Annie noticed that her
mother looked relieved. The muscles on her forehead
were strangely smooth and relaxed.

"How are you doing, Mom?"

"I'm really doing fine, Annie." Aunt Patti joined them
in the kitchen. Patti's eyes were red and her face was
puffy.

Her mother continued," I know I have some tough
times ahead of me, but I'm glad the funeral and everything is over. I'm sure I'm going to be fine."

Patti sat silently at the table staring at the cup of
coffee Mrs. McDonald put in front of her. Annie stood
behind her aunt and rubbed her shoulders.

"Bud went to pick up Gwen," Mrs. McDonald continued brightly. "We can all have breakfast together,
and then we have a few things we need to talk about
before you have to head back, Annie. Mrs. Thompson
brought us an egg and cheese strata." She took the
casserole from the refrigerator and put it in the oven,

then poured Annie a glass of orange juice. "So did you and Jayne and Mebo catch up with each other?"

"We sure did, Mom," Annie drained her juice. "We stayed up too late, though. We promised to stay in touch with each other."

"You should get together more often. You girls went through a lot together, and it would be a shame to lose touch."

In that instant Annie realized that her mother understood a lot more than she'd ever given her credit for.

"Mrs. Thompson suggested that I take golf lessons with her this summer," Annie's mother giggled. "You know, I think I will."

Patti looked scornfully at her sister-in-law.

"Patti, you said yourself that I should keep busy, and Mrs. Thompson has been so nice to me through all of this. And when you go home Patti, I'll need something to keep my mind off things," Annie's mother explained.

"I think that sounds really great, Mom," Annie was pleasantly surprised that her mother was becoming a real person, and finally doing something for herself.

Bud and Gwen came laughing into the kitchen holding hands. Annie wondered if it was her imagination or if there was suddenly a light-hearted, almost warm feeling in this house. The smell of cigars was fading fast. Only Aunt Patti showed signs of mourning.

Patti disappeared into the guest room and minutes later returned carrying her suitcase. "Polly, I think I'll be leaving now. You all seem to be doing fine and I'll leave you to your family gathering. You don't need me here."

"Oh, Patti, are you sure you don't want to have brunch with us?" Annie's mother hoped Patti wasn't feeling neglected.

"No, Dears, it's time I get back to my life and leave you to yours," she softly replied.

"Bye, Aunt Salmon Patti," Annie gave her aunt a big hug and a kiss. "Thank you for being here for us, you old sweetie."

"Where else would I have been?" Patti was close to tears.

"Good-bye, Patti, and thanks for everything," Bud put his arms around his aunt. "Come back to see us again real soon. Remember, there's going to be a wedding in the fall."

"My little Buddy getting married," Patti squeezed Bud's arm. "I only wish your dad could have been here for the big event." She then glanced over to Gwen.

Annie thought to herself, "Well, maybe not."

Patti walked over to Gwen, gave her a little hug and whispered, "You and Bud be happy, okay? I'll be back for this big wedding."

Gwen was speechless and smiled at Patti. Bud had already picked up Patti's suitcase and was heading for the front door.

"Now, Polly, you call me if you need me, and I'll drop *everything* to be here for you." Patti put her ecru crocheted purse under her right arm and gave Annie's mother a hug with her left.

"I'll be fine Patti, but I really couldn't have made it through this weekend without you. You're a saint." Annie's mother walked her to the door. As Patti's car backed out of the drive, Annie heard a small sigh of relief from her mother. The moment the car was off the property, Annie's mother exclaimed in a light, happy tone, "Let's have brunch!"

Annie decided she liked her "new" mom. Even Bud seemed different. He was more attentive to Gwen than he had been when Annie first met her. They sat with Annie and their mother in the kitchen and happily discussed wedding plans. They were to be married in October and asked Annie to be one of the attendants. Annie's mom was enjoying all the planning and volunteered to help in any way should could.

"Mom, I think we'll drive Ruby for a while, but then I'll probably try to sell her. We'll need a bigger car when we start our family, and we'd like to get going on that soon." Gwen blushed at Bud's comments. "Do you think that will be okay?"

"Of course, Bud," Annie's mom replied. "I gave that old truck to you and Gwen. You can do whatever you want with it. It has no sentimental value for me. You know, Bud, we really should get your father's ashes out of the truck. He loved Ruby, but I hardly think that it's appropriate for the two of you to be driving around town with the urn hanging from the back window."

Annie's mother was suddenly a little more solemn, but Annie laughed out loud.

"I'm sorry, Mom," she explained. "But I forgot all about the urn still being in the truck. I guess we'd better decide what to do with it."

All of them saw the bizarre humor in Butch's cremains riding around in the truck. Her mother shook her head at them and tried to act offended, but the twinkle in her eye didn't match the scowl on her mouth.

"Do either of you kids have any suggestions about a final resting place?"

Mr. Holvey had asked Annie's mother what her plans were for Mr. McDonald's cremains and she didn't know how to reply. She knew that she didn't want to keep them in the house. She didn't even want to see the urn, let along touch it. She told Mr. Holvey that the family would decide about that later and asked Bud to put them in Ruby for a while since Butch was so fond of the truck.

"Mom," Annie had a plan. "Would it be all right with all of you if I scattered Dad's ashes? I would like to be alone and I would very much like to take the ashes to the river. You know how he loved to go over there, park Ruby on the bank and fish for hours at a time. Don't you think that sounds like the perfect resting place?"

"That *would* be perfect, Annie. Are you sure you want to be alone?" Her mother seemed concerned.

"I really need to say good-bye in my own way, Mom. You do understand don't you?" Annie's gaze shifted between her mother and Bud. She was asking for permission to do this from both of them. "Would it be all right with you if I took Ruby out for a while?"

"It's fine with me, Annie," Bud nodded. "You can have the truck as long as you want it. We can take Mom's car if we need to go anywhere." Bud rubbed Annie's back, and for the first time in years, Annie was glad that she had a little brother.

Annie's mother was clearing the table, and she poured Annie another cup of coffee. "Annie, I'll be here all day, so whenever you come back home is fine with me. We can talk before you have to head back to the airport. What time is your flight?"

"Not 'til 8:15, Mom. I'll be back in plenty of time to visit before I have to go," Annie took a sip of the coffee and asked Bud for the keys to Ruby. "See you guys later," Annie said as she stood. "This was a great family brunch, Mom."

Annie could feel a familiar twinge in her stomach as she approached the truck, but jumped in behind the steering wheel in spite of it. The silver urn had two handles, like ears sticking out from its sides. One of the handles was looped over the hook of the gun rack so that it hung just behind Annie's head. "This has got to change, Dad," she said as she unhooked the urn and moved it to the hook on the passenger side.

She noticed that Bud had taped the lid onto the urn to keep it from spilling. "Classy as ever," Annie said as she backed the truck out of the drive.

"I have the perfect place for you, Dad," Annie headed out of Dodge toward the river. There was an evil edge to her voice. "Yes, Dad, yesterday Jayne and Mebo and I prepared an appropriate final resting place for you on our way back from Keokuk. We went to The Dock, Dad. Did you know that it was a gay bar now?" Annie snickered. She was enjoying the absolute control she had over her father.

"Too bad you couldn't have met your daughter-in-law-to-be," Annie reached over with her right hand and patted the urn. "She's really a lovely girl, Dad. Did I mention that she's Black?"

Annie drove too fast. She was quiet for a minute, and when she spoke again, her tone was different. "You bigoted pervert. I'm glad you're gone. I really am. Do you know what we did today? We had a family brunch. Bud and Gwen and Mom and I sat down and had a very pleasant meal for the first time in our lives because *you weren't there!*"

She came to the intersection she was looking for and turned onto the country road. She pulled off onto the soft shoulder and jammed on the brakes. She was aware that her father always drove Ruby very carefully.

"I told Mom that I was going to scatter your ashes in the river. Well, we're not quite to the river. But last night there was a *little* river in this ditch, Dad," she unhooked the urn from the gun rack and opened the door. The urn felt small to her and too light.

She stepped down out of the truck and stood by the

ditch that had served as an emergency ladies' room on the way back from Keokuk last night and pulled the tape off the lid of the urn. She expected the contents to smell of stale cigars but, when she sniffed, it had no odor.

Suddenly she wondered what she was doing. She thought about her mother and the hope she had seen in her eyes this morning. Hope for a peaceful remainder of her life.

Annie looked at the urn she held in her hands. She thought about her ability to empty it in the impromptu toilet or throw it in the corn field on the other side of the ditch. Somehow, just knowing that she could do whatever she wanted to with the urn and its contents took away the need to do it.

She stood there for several minutes before she realized that she was crying. "Why couldn't you have been a good father to me? I wanted you to love me so much, Dad," she clutched the urn to her chest and leaned against the truck. "You hurt me. You used me and made me feel dirty and worthless." The sobs racked her body. It seemed as if she would never be able to stop crying.

Slowly, slowly the sobbing subsided until she was standing silently again. She was intent on searching her memories. "One time … one time when I was eight or nine, you brought me fishing. Just you and I drove to the river and you helped me. I caught a catfish. You laughed when I cried because I was afraid the hook had stuck the fish in its neck. I squealed as you helped me pull if from the water. 'Catfish have no necks', you said, and you beamed at me. That one time you were proud of me, and I was so happy when we brought it home."

She sighed and slowly got back into the truck. She sat the urn on the passenger side and fastened the seat belt around it to hold it securely upright. Annie cranked the steering wheel, turned the truck around on the gravel road, and headed toward the river.

She drove in silence to a parking area where two other trucks were parked. She parked Ruby far away from the other trucks, the way her father would have. As she unfastened the seat belt around the urn, she thought about losing the father she never really had and felt the sadness deep within her.

She walked to the edge of the river holding the urn gingerly and sat down on the bank. "The old Mississippi is the only place you were ever proud of me. I never could please you, Dad, but this I can do for you. I can give you a decent burial. One you would approve of."

She removed the lid from the urn and scattered the contents into the muddy river. Tiny bits of ash that looked like sand sank into the water. Others floated and were soon carried by the current out toward the center of the mighty river. Sea gulls called and glided overhead and Annie noticed that it was a beautiful day.

The reeds growing near the bank swayed slightly in the breeze and puffy, white clouds reflected on the smooth water. To her right, about a hundred yards away, a father stood fishing with his little boy. The boy yelled with delight when his bobber disappeared under the surface.

"Good-bye, Daddy," Annie wiped a tear from her cheek and walked back to the truck.

Annie was wonderfully at peace when she returned to her mother's house. She found her mother resting on the couch in the living room. Annie set the empty urn on the mantle.

Her mother rose and put her arms around Annie. Annie returned the embrace and they stood there comforting each other silently for a while.

"Were you able to say good-bye?" her mother asked gently.

Annie nodded and smiled at her mother, "Where are Bud and Gwen?"

"They walked up to the Square. Bud wanted to show her the town."

"Had you met Gwen before, Mom?" Annie found it easy to talk with her mother now.

"I met Gwen for the first time about a year ago. Of course, your father never met her," her mother continued. "I think Gwen has a lot of patience, putting up with that. She really is a lovely girl."

"Mom, do you need anything?" Are you okay for money?"

"Money was something that your father was pretty good at." Mrs. McDonald patted her daughter's hand.

"He had a good insurance policy and I'll get his pension from work, so I'll be fine. In fact, I plan on doing some things I've always wanted to do. I might even get to New York one of these times and you and I can paint the town."

"Oh, Mom, that would be wonderful," Annie laughed. "Yes, I think you will be just fine."

Gwen and Bud came in the back door laughing. The four of them spent the afternoon talking about wedding plans. Gwen talked about her family who had finally accepted Bud. Annie agreed that Gwen and Bud seemed happy together.

"What about you, Annie? Seeing someone special?" Bud winked at his sister, and she told them a little about Patrick.

The afternoon passed quickly. They said their good-byes, and Bud left to take Gwen home.

Annie reached for her mother's hands. "I have to get going, too, Mom."

"I know you do. I'm so glad to see you happy, Annie," she said with tears glistening in her eyes. "Before you go would you do one last thing for me?"

"Of course, Mom, what do you want?"

Her mother bit her bottom lip and asked, "Would you take that damn deer head off the wall and put it by the curb? Tomorrow is garbage day."

Think

ARETHA FRANKLIN

You better think
(think, think)
About what you're trying to do to me.

Mebo let herself into the quiet house. The porch light and the kitchen light were on. She slipped off her shoes inside the kitchen and tiptoed into the nursery. In the glow of the night light, Mebo watched Beebee sleeping. The baby had kicked off her blanket, and it lay in a crumpled heap at the foot of the crib. Beebee's right arm hugged a ragged, pink bunny, and her left thumb was securely in her mouth. Mebo softly touched the baby's silky hair, and Beebee gave her thumb a few quick tugs in response.

Silent tears welled up in Mebo's eyes, and she thought her heart would burst with love for the baby. She carefully tiptoed up the stairs and peeked in on the boys. The blinds were pulled up, and a cool breeze blew through the open window. The pole light outside lit the room. Benny lay on his stomach on the bottom bunk. His left arm and leg were slung over the side of the bed. His pillow was on the floor ready to cushion his head when he fell out of bed as he often did.

She smiled to think that the regular occurrence never woke him. Brad slept completely covered by the sheet. He had slept with his head under the covers all his life.

She quietly crossed the hall and pushed open the door to the twins' room. Bella's half of the room was perfectly neat and Betsy's half was strewn with clothes and clutter.

As Mebo crept back downstairs, she mused that this was the way things should be. All her children were sleeping peacefully. They all were secure and happy individuals.

She pulled off her jeans and t-shirt in the bathroom and slipped into the nightgown that hung on the hook on the door, then tiptoed into her room. Bob reached his arm around her instinctively as she slipped in beside him. She was asleep in minutes.

Mebo didn't wake up until 9:30 Sunday morning. The house was quiet and it took her a minute to get oriented. She dragged herself out of bed and smelled coffee. She followed the smell into the kitchen.

"Where is everyone?" she called out to the empty house. She looked out the back door and saw that the car was gone. She poured herself a cup of coffee and sat down at the table. There, leaning against the sugar bowl, was a note written on the back of an envelope.

Mom—

Betsy and I took the kids to church. Dad's in

the field. Hope we didn't wake you.

Love Bella.

Mebo read the note three times. When she stood to refill her coffee she was awake enough to look around the house and realized that things were odd.

"The house is still clean!" she said out loud. "I leave Bob and the kids for a whole day and come home to find a clean house and wake up to find fresh coffee waiting for me. What's wrong with this picture?"

She decided to fix a real Sunday dinner for her family—fried chicken, mashed potatoes and gravy, vegetables and hot rolls—the whole bit. The clean house and the peace and quiet inspired her. She was busily frying chicken when she heard the car drive in.

The kids bounded through the door in a flood of noise and laughter.

"Hi, Mom," Brad was the first one to appear in the kitchen.

"Hey, Mommy sleepy head," Benny was jumping across the floor in his new church shoes. His little bow tie was on crooked and his shirt tail was sticking out, but he looked perfect to Mebo.

"Hi, my babies, how was Mass?" she gave the boys a group hug.

"Okay, I guess," Benny replied. "You missed it."

"Boring as usual," Brad said as he pulled off his tie. "Fried chicken, awesome!"

The twins walked into the room, and Bella handed the baby to her mother, "How you doing, Mom? Have fun last night?"

Betsy chimed in, "Did you stay out all night?"

"I really had a great time with Jayne and Annie. It was like old times and yes, we talked most of the night. How did everything go here? The house looks great." Mebo was playing with the baby's hair and holding her close to her chest.

"Yeah, we all straightened up around here before we went to bed last night," Bella said. "With all of us working it didn't take long."

"Dad cleaned up the kitchen. He made us spaghetti for supper," Betsy added. "It wasn't that bad."

Mebo handed the baby back to Bella and asked her to go change the wet diaper. She looked over at Bob, who was standing in the doorway. Mebo smiled, "Hi, how ya doing?"

Bob's face registered no emotion, "How should I be?"

"I decided to make fried chicken for Sunday dinner. Are you hungry?" She turned toward the sizzling frying pan on the stove.

Bob stumbled over Benny's dress shoes and caught himself on the door to the bathroom. "Damn, it, Briget, it's not bad enough that you're out all night the least you can do is pick up around here."

Mebo caught herself starting to feel guilty then she remembered her recaptured strength. She straightened and returned her attention to making dinner.

The children had all disappeared into their rooms. "Hang up your church clothes," Mebo called from the bottom of the stairs. When she returned to the kitchen, Bob was waiting for her.

"Out drinking all night?" he barked.

She noticed how scared he looked when his face was red.

"What kind of an example is that for your kids? It's okay, for Jayne and Fannie, but you've got kids and a husband to think about—"

She didn't wait for him to finish his tirade. "What kind of an example?" She echoed him with such calm power and surety that it surprised Mebo almost as much as it surprised Bob. "I'll tell you what kind of example I'm going to be from now on. I'm going to be an example of confidence and self-respect."

She felt much taller as she turned back to the task of frying chicken. Bob was agape. Mebo thought that this must be one of his biggest nightmares, and she smiled wryly at the concept.

"Listen, Missy," Bob, in his usual masculine style, responded to this perceived threat with increased volume. "You can't talk to me like—"

"Pardon me?" Mebo felt as if she had just broken free of shackles, and if felt good. "I can't talk to you like that?" She was still in control of her voice. "Just how in the Hell do you think you've been talking to me for the past year?" She was on a roll.

Mebo noticed that the twins and Brad were standing in the door of the kitchen. Brad looked confused and a little scared, but Mebo thought that she read the faintest hint of approval on the girls' faces.

Bob looked as if he had been hit by a truck. He tried to say something. His face was dark red and Mebo wondered if he was about to have a stroke. Instead, he stomped out, slamming the door behind him.

Mebo realized that even good changes would be difficult for the kids. She didn't know for sure if Bob was coming back today, but she knew that either way, before the day was over she was going to have a long talk with the kids.

"Yes, there are going to be some changes made around here," she thought. "We're in for the ride of our lives, and it's about time."

"It appears that your father has decided not to join us for dinner," Mebo announced to her children.

The First Time Ever I Saw Your Face

ROBERTA FLACK

The first time ever I lay with you,
I felt your heart so close to mine.

Jayne woke late Sunday morning to the piercing sound of gunfire. It took her a while to realize that she was in her old bedroom in Dodge, and that in reality Mr. Ginster's lawn mower was backfiring. When she rolled over, her pounding head reminded her that she had too much to drink last night—something that she was not in the habit of doing. She looked over to the twin bed beside her to see if Annie was awake, but found the bed already made, with a note on the pillow.

Flashbacks of the night before filled her head. The Three had all said their good-byes last night. It had been an exhausting two days, but Jayne felt good about them. She was glad she came home, but she was also eager to get back to Des Moines.

She pulled herself out of bed and headed for the

bathroom, reading Annie's note on the way. She fumbled through the medicine cabinet until she found a bottle of aspirin, took two, and turned on the shower. She let the water run over her face and body for a long time. It felt great, and she was renewed.

She dressed quickly, threw her clothes together in her suitcase, and went downstairs to find her mother. She thought maybe she would have a quick cup of coffee and hit the road. Her life in Des Moines was waiting for her.

She found her mom sitting on the deck reading the Sunday paper, still dressed in the clothes she wore to church. Jayne poured herself a cup of coffee and went out to join her.

"Good morning," Jayne sang out through the screen door.

"Hi, dear. Did you girls find some coffee?" her mother said, looking up from her paper. Jayne mused that her mother may as well not read the paper, since she was sure that she only read the pleasant parts.

"I did," Jayne replied as she found a chair in the sun. "Annie already left while you were at church. She left a note and thanked us for everything. She said to tell you good-bye."

"I'm sorry I missed her," Jayne's mother said, putting down the newspaper and looking over at Jayne. "Did you have fun last night? I didn't hear you come in."

"We really did have a good time. We decided to get

together more often."

Her mother smiled her approval.

"You'll never guess who we ran into last night. We went to Sigley to eat tenderloins. You know Ramsey's has the best in the world. Anyway, we saw Peter."

Mrs. Lipton's face brightened. "Oh, Peter," she said with cautious nostalgia. "I haven't seen him for years. Do his parents still live in Sigley?"

"Yes. Peter was there with his son. He's divorced and his son loves to visit his grandparents."

"Well, I think that they are lucky people to have a grandchild." Mrs. Lipton didn't try to hide the point. They were interrupted by the telephone.

"I'll get it for you." Jayne sprang from her chair and ran into the family room, planning on bringing the cordless phone back out to her mother. When Jayne didn't reappear, her mother went back to her paper.

"Liptons."

"Jayne?" The sound of Peter's voice dissolved the years. She forgot to answer. "Jayne?" He sounded more tentative.

"Yes," her voice was too high. "Yes," she tried to correct the pitch and immediately realized how foolish she sounded.

"Um, this is Peter."

They both laughed at their inability to get past greetings.

"Yeah, I know ... um ..." Jayne willed herself to not laugh uncontrollably as she had done so often this weekend. She decided to do something even if it was wrong. "I know," she said with a decisive air. "Let's just start this whole phone call over."

"Good idea!" Peter sounded relieved. "Pretend like you are just answering the phone."

"Liptons," Jayne sang into the receiver with an exaggerated lilt.

"Hello, Darlin'!" he said, sounding like a country-western singer. "What say we have lunch at Ramsay's and pick up where we left off about … twenty years ago?"

Jayne was speechless.

"Oh, sorry," said Peter. "Look, just have lunch with me, okay? I don't know how to ask seventeen year-olds out anymore."

"You never were much good at it." Jayne was dangerously near giggling. "Asking girls out, that is." She was sure he heard her blushing.

"Look," Peter sounded no-nonsense now, "You'd better just say when you'll meet me at Ramsey's before we get in any more trouble here."

"Right. How about 1:00?"

"Great. See you then. Good-bye, Jayne."

"Good-bye, Chessie Cat." Jayne had hung up the phone before she realized the significance of what she'd done.

Twenty years ago she called him Chessie Cat because she said his smile warmed her even after he'd left the room. She didn't realize that she even remembered that silly little name. It was as if her brain forgot it, but her soul did not. "Get it together, Girl." Jayne shook her head sharply. "You don't know anything about him." She said it aloud, hoping that she'd believe it.

"Did you say something, Jayney?" her mother called from the deck.

"Speak of the Devil!" Jayne spoke with all the non-chalance she could muster as she rejoined her mother. "That was Peter. He's going to buy me lunch in beautiful, downtown Sigley on my way home."

"How nice!" Her mother's eyes searched her face. "But you better watch out. Two men are one too many."

"It's just lunch, Mom," Jayne laughed but she knew better. Mother and daughter talked for an hour in the sunshine.

"You are great, Mom," Jayne beamed at her mother. "You always make Mebo and Annie feel so much at home."

"Oh, I just love those girls," her mother replied.

"I'd better get going. I have some things to do at home and I am already going to be late for my big lunch date." She winked at her mother.

On the way to Sigley, Jayne thought about the past weekend, the past twenty years ... and even the next twenty. The past two days had been a roller coaster ride, but overall it was the best trip back to Dodge she'd ever had. And she couldn't help thinking that it could be even better.

When she drove into Sigley she felt her heart beating faster. She had so much trouble just talking to him on the phone, the thought of having lunch alone with him was electric.

"Relax!" she ordered herself. "He's just a guy you used to know. Maybe talking with him will make you realize that he is just an ordinary person and not the perfect man that you think you remember." Even as she said the words, she knew they weren't true.

She parked the car in front of Ramsey's Café for the second time in as many days. She realized that a strange woman in the café two days in a row would constitute a major news item in Sigley. She saw Peter sitting at the table by the window where they had sat the night before.

"Hi." He stood and took her hands when she walked up to the table. "I was afraid you weren't coming." His eyes didn't release her.

The lunch crowd consisted of about fifteen people, filling the place, and every one of them watched the couple.

"Mom and I started talking, and I lost track of time," Jayne explained. "You know how I am."

Peter blushed at the implication of her remark, "I know how you are."

Jayne reclaimed her hands, tore herself from his gaze and sat down. Even though she reasoned that no one in the café knew who she was or would probably ever see her again, their stares made her uncomfortable. The same pimply waitress appeared at their table and grinned silently with her green pad and pencil poised and ready.

"I'd like a tenderloin and fries," Peter said, then looked at Jayne. "Me, too."

"Oh, and two Green Rivers," Peter said to the waitress without taking his eyes off Jayne's.

The first time they made love, Peter had planned a perfect, romantic night for them. It all came rushing back to her. He had taken everything for a picnic dinner to his family's river house. He had spent weeks planning every last detail. He had goose liver pâte, baguettes, green grapes, brie, and a bottle of Beringer Chardonnay. It was an unseasonably cool, clear day in early September, the weekend before he went away to college. A fire was prepared, and in front of the fireplace he had spread a soft, blue blanket.

He made her close her eyes and led her up the stone steps to the cabin. She trembled then when he kissed her cheek and whispered to her to open her eyes. She trembled now remembering it.

"Don't get crazy on me," Jayne thought and she mentally recited some other facts about that first night. They both thought the pâte smelled like cat food. The floor was cold, in spite of the fire and the blankets, and although he remembered plenty of contraception, Peter forgot to bring a corkscrew.

He was determined that the evening not be a disaster. He scavenged around in the little kitchen and found one bottle of Green River soda that his father had left from a fishing trip earlier that summer.

They forgot about the cold.

"It would be criminal to come here and not eat the tenderloins," Jayne didn't' know what to say.

"What *would* be criminal," Peter leaned toward her, "would be if we didn't order Green Rivers." His blue eyes bore into Jayne, and she felt herself blush. She silently chided herself for acting like an adolescent.

"Look, Jayne," he began, "for years, I've been thinking about what I would say to you if I ever got the chance. I don't want to blow it now. So forgive me if I get straight to the point."

Jayne's palms were damp and she could feel her heart pounding out a warning.

"I knew when I was breaking up with you that I would live to regret it. I knew you were special, and that I probably would never find anyone I cared about as deeply." Jayne's head was spinning as he continued, "Even though I was older, you were much more mature than I was. Sometimes I think you were born mature. Always level-headed."

"I sure don't feel very level headed now, Peter."

"I knew that if we stayed together and got married as we'd planned, that I would always wonder. I needed to date other people. I really needed to. But I always thought we'd get back together." He shook his head in disgust. "That proves how foolish I was. I thought you'd just be waiting for me. I knew I was making a mistake at the time, but not dating other people would have been a mistake, too." His words were flooding out. "By the time I was brave enough to tell you, you were married."

The waitress appeared with their sandwiches. Jayne glanced up to see the people at the next table staring at them, obviously listening to Peter's confession.

"I ... I just wanted you to know that. I didn't want you to think that I didn't value you. I truly loved you, Jayne."

Jayne sat dumbfounded, staring at her tenderloin as if it had just flown in from Pluto. "Well!" It was the only word she could find for a while.

There it was. The speech she'd wanted to hear for twenty years. She looked across the table and studied Peter's face. His face was flushed with red, and tiny beads of sweat dotted his forehead. His sandy hair was messed up by his nervous habit of running his hands through it. His blue eyes were focused on her face, and all she could think of was how badly she wanted to wipe the dampness from his face.

"You certainly know how to sweep a girl off her feet!"

He smiled at her timidly. "I'm sorry, but I was afraid if I didn't say all that now, I'd never have another chance. You look wonderful, by the way."

She tore her eyes away from his. "I think this stuff is getting cold." They took bites of their food, but it was obvious to everyone in the café that they only had an appetite for each other.

Peter glanced around the room and people went

back to their lunches. "Let's get out of here and go somewhere we can talk," he whispered. "Mom and Dad have taken Seth to see his great-grandma for the day."

"I don't know, Peter," Jayne said softly, "I think you're talking pretty well in here."

He beamed at her and raised his eyebrows in a question. "I have some champagne and Green Rivers cooling."

The smile faded from Peter's eyes and Jayne nearly changed her mind. "I need some time to digest all of this."

They both looked at their lunches, which had two bites missing, and laughed.

"I mean I need some time to think." She sat for a minute while Peter paid the check, then they walked to her car together. Jayne pulled another business card and a pen from her purse. She wrote her home phone number on the card and gave it to him. "Why don't we both go home? If you still want to talk in a week or two, call me."

She got into her car and rolled down the window. He bent over to look in and smiled his Cheshire Cat smile. His eyes were misty.

"I'll call you next week," he leaned in through the window, kissed her lightly on the lips and walked off toward his parent's house.

Suddenly she realized that psychology wasn't the only thing she'd been practicing for the past ten years. She had been practicing telling herself that her body was a traitor when she trembled at the thought of Green Rivers or cried at the mention of a Cheshire Cat. She practiced telling herself that she had romanticized her memories of Peter, and that their relationship was just some adolescent angst being worked out. She practiced being practical and sensible. And suddenly she felt like a fool.

When she reached the city limits of Sigley, without so much as a glance in the rear-view mirror, she threw her sterile objectivity out the window. She slammed on the brakes, backed onto the shoulder, cranked the wheel, and sped directly to Peter's parents' house throwing gravel behind her. She pulled into the driveway just as he reached the back door.

Undun

THE GUESS WHO

And when I found what she was headed for,
It was too late.

Annie struggled with the deer head, but got it to the curb. She left it face down because the staring glass eyes gave her the creeps. Then, as an afterthought, she went back into the house and asked her mother if she could use the phone to check her messages.

"Of course, Honey, go ahead." Her mother peeked through the curtains and shook her head at the remains of her late husband's one successful hunting trip.

Annie called her answering machine to see if there was anything she needed to handle by phone before she got home. There were two calls from Patrick telling her he missed her, a call from a friend at work expressing condolences, two hang-ups, and a call from Justice.

"Annie, it's me," even though she immediately recognized his voice, there was an icy quality about it now and it chilled her to the bone. "Did you have a good reunion? Just wanted you to know that my next call will be to Patrick. I'm also delivering a very special video to his office today. I made you a star, Babe. I think he'll be surprised at some of the tricks you know. By the time you get home you'll be left with no one. Just the way The Three left my mother. Remember Sarah? You've all paid now."

Annie felt her stomach sink when she listened to the message for the second time. Her heart was racing and she felt the blood rush to her face. There wasn't enough air in the room to fill her lungs.

"His mother … Sarah!" The words echoed inside her head. "This has got to be some kind of sick joke," even as she mumbled the words, she knew that it wasn't.

Like lightening came the realization that her Justice was also Mebo's farmhand and Jayne's patient. They *had* all paid. She felt faint and was seeing white spots as she dialed the phone. It seemed forever until Jayne's machine answered.

"Jayne," she was aware that her voice portrayed her panic. "Call me as soon as you get this message."

The shaking only worsened as she dialed Mebo's number. Mebo picked up on the second ring. "Mebo, you better sit down."

Diary

BREAD

The words she's written took me by surprise—
You'd never read them in her eyes.

December 27, 1973

Today I'll begin this diary as I
begin my new life with Justice Robert
Simpson. I finally have a family of my
very own and no matter what, Justice
will always know he's loved and he
belongs.

He weighs just over seven pounds and
is twenty inches long. He has a lot of
black hair and clear gray eyes like his
father.

It's impossible to imagine that I
ever considered not having this baby.
Justice is all mine and his father will
never get to share him. I gave him a
chance seven months ago and he made it
clear that he wanted no part of us. He
doesn't deserve us.

March 28, 1974

This is the one year anniversary of
Justice's conception. Somehow it was
the best and the worst day of my life.
Annie set me up. She pretended to be my
friend that night the way Bob pretended
to care about me. I hate them both for
that, but at the same time if it hadn't
happened the way it did, I never would
have Justice -- my life. I could never
regret that.

May 30, 1974

The anniversary of the Last Fling.
All I ever wanted was to be a part of
Annie, Briget and Jayne's friendship.
But I never really understood why that
was so important to me. It was as if
I needed to be part of their group in
order to be whole. But they wouldn't
even acknowledge me. I went to Chicago,
too. The Three were so hung up on
themselves that they didn't even notice
me the times I was driving right behind
them. Just the way they never noticed
me at school.

February 19, 1976

Justice loves pancakes!! I took a
picture of him sitting in his high
chair with pancakes and syrup smeared
all over him. I wonder if his hair
will ever get clean. It doesn't matter.
Seeing him so happy is worth it. Surely
Briget and Bob can't be this happy. They
should rot in Hell. Surely what goes
around comes around. Believing that
makes me think that someday justice
will be served.

Hotel California

THE EAGLES

You can check out any time you like,
But you can never leave.

Justice walked into Kailin Center for what he knew would be the last time. Earlier today the charge nurse on his mother's floor had finally gotten in touch with him. His machine had been blinking when he entered his meager studio apartment. He had been busy performing his final act of revenge and had been out of town a lot. His obsession didn't even leave room for him to check his messages during his brief times at home. Now he felt guilty because the staff at Kailin had been trying to reach him to tell him that his mother was failing and wasn't expected to live much longer.

For the first time—and the last—Justice stood in the middle of his apartment and looked around. The plaster was crumbling and the place smelled of mildew. The sheet he hung over the only window had fallen down in one corner and was stained from rain and dust. The sink and chipped bathtub were both stained dark orange-brown and the cord that held the light bulb that dangled from the ceiling was frayed. The only nice place in the apartment was a table he kept as a shrine. It was covered with white linen and pictures of him and his mother in silver frames were placed between silver candlesticks. A cedar box with a carved ivory rose held his mother's diaries. Spread before them were four well-worn pages taken from the diaries that he believed contained the instructions of revenge from his mother.

He packed the contents of the shrine into a duffel bag that also held his meager wardrobe.

It wasn't going to be hard to leave a place like this. Even though the apartment he had shared with his mother on the other side of town had been modest, she had always made it feel like home. It was clean and neat.

Before he could reach his mother's doorway, a familiar third-shift nurse interceded with a gentle touch to his arm. Later, he realized that his mind had tried its best to protect him from the news she shared. All the while she spoke, his eyes scanned from her crooked eye glasses to her chunky, white shoes.

"She looks just right to be telling me this bad news," he thought. She was soft. Her voice sounded soft, her flesh looked soft. She even smelled of softly scented soap.

The soft nurse said, "I want to prepare you for your mother's condition. She had another stroke two weeks ago. It's really just a matter of days, maybe hours. She's being kept alive by a respirator now. We thought that we would lose her for sure last week, but she held on."

"She held on to see me again and to know that I had completed her plans," he mumbled.

He realized that the staff who had taken care of her for the past couple of years thought he was a bit of an odd character. "They probably think that insanity runs in the family," he thought. He didn't care what they thought of him as long as they took good care of his mother. He knew that neither of them were crazy. They just needed to even the score. They needed justice.

He took a deep breath and entered the dingy, half-lit room. The room smelled strongly of disinfectant and some other smell. "The smell of death," he thought.

Even with the preparation from the nurse, the sight of his mother hooked up to wires and tubes, and the sound of the respirator made him freeze. "Could I open the window a bit, please," he asked.

"I don't see what that would hurt," the nurse replied. She gently touched his arm again.

"She doesn't understand," he thought, "that my mother's impending death is not a bad thing."

"I'll leave you alone with her," whispered the nurse as she left the room.

Justice pulled the only chair in the room close to the bed and held the dying woman's tiny hand in his.

"When did you get so small, Mother? You were always so strong when I was growing up. Well, you gave me your strength, and I have finished what you planned years ago. It's all done now, Mother, and now you can go to your peace. I know you left the diary for me to find. I did just what you wanted me to do."

"First, there was Jayne. She never included you— none of them did. But Jayne always was perceived as a saint. Some saint."

As he continued his mother remained motionless, except for an occasional twitch of her eyelid. Justice knew that she understood everything he was saying.

"I made her pay, Mother. She spent years building up her practice in Minneapolis. Imagine *her* being a psychologist. Psychologists are supposed to help people. Well, she doesn't have the practice there anymore. I made sure of that."

He gently stroked her brittle hair. "Then there was Mebo. This one was the hardest because I had to live and work with that asshole father of mine. I'm afraid she and that monster had a terrible fire. They trusted me the way you trusted them, and their dreams went up in smoke the way yours did so many years ago. He was so proud of his precious children and he wouldn't even acknowledge having another child somewhere."

Justice noticed that he had warmed his mother's hand in his. For several minutes the only sounds were the respirator and a woman down the hall singing the first two lines of "Amazing Grace" over and over again.

He smiled wryly at his mother, "And just yesterday, I completed our plans. That bitch, Annie, is about to find out how it feels to get the rug pulled out from under her. Tender moments between Annie and me have been captured forever on video tape." His smile broadened and his steely, gray eyes flashed as he went on. "She made sure you'd never find a man to love you. Well I made sure that she'll lose the man she loves."

"It's all right now, Mother," he stroked her hair while he sat silently at her bedside. "It's all okay. Justice has been served."

He didn't notice the owl staring at him through the open window from a treetop.

He stood and leaned over to kiss her pasty cheek. "Rest now, Mother. Rest."

Justice reached above and behind her bed, and, with one solitary tear on his cheek, unplugged the respirator.

The owl flew into the night.

Epilogue

Sometimes the friendships we make in childhood are the strongest. We even learn to run to the safe harbor of our childhood friends to weather our adult storms. What we learn from each other we take to our adult relationships.

Perhaps The Three had even more going for them than that. With confidence borrowed from each other, one redefined her place in a marriage, one let down her barrier of cool detachment enough to rekindle a love from long ago, and one gave herself permission to love a man who loves her enough to overlook infidelity.

Perhaps the monsters are gone from every place except their memories. And with their friends, they might learn to handle even those.

Table of Referenced Songs & Lyrics

WITCHY WOMAN

Performer	The Eagles
Album	Eagles
Label	Asylum
Writers	Don Henley, Bernie Leadon
Producer	Glyn Johns

TAKE ME HOME, COUNTRY ROADS

Performer	John Denver
Album	Poems, Prayers and Promises
Label	RCA
Writers	John Denver, Bill Danoff, Taffy Nivert
Producers	Milton Okun, Susan Ruskin

BAD MOON RISING

Performer	Creedence Clearwater Revival
Album	Green River
Label	Fantasy
Writer, Producer	John Fogerty

HELP!

Performer	The Beatles
Album	Help!
Label	Parlophone, Capitol Records
Writers	John Lennon, Paul McCartney
Producer	George Martin

GOIN' OUT OF MY HEAD

Performer	Dionne Warwick
Album	Very Dionne
Label	Scepter Records
Writers	Teddy Randazzo, Bobby Weinstein
Producer	Burt Bacharach

STAND BY ME

Performer	Ben E. King
Album	Don't Play That Song!
Label	Atco
Writers	Ben E. King, Jerry Leiber, Mike Stoller
Producer	Ben E. King

GREAT PRETENDER

Performer	Platters
Label	Mercury Records
Writer, Producer	Buck Ram

DREAMS OF THE EVERYDAY HOUSEWIFE

Performer	Glen Campbell
Album	Wichita Linemen
Label	Capitol
Writer	Chris Gantry
Producer	Al DeLory

STAND BY YOUR MAN
Performer	Tammy Wynette
Label	Epic
Writers	Billy Sherrill, Tammy Wynette
Producer	Billy Sherrill

SO FAR AWAY
Performer	Carole King
Album	Tapestry
Label	Ode
Writer	Carole King
Producer	Lou Adler

OH, PRETTY WOMAN
Performer	Roy Orbison
Label	Monument
Writers	Roy Orbison, Bill Dees
Producer	Fred Foster

YOU DON'T OWN ME
Performer	Lesley Gore
Album	Lesley Gore Sings of Mixed-Up Hearts
Label	Mercury
Writers	John Madara, Dave White
Producer	Quincy Jones

NA NA, HEY HEY, KISS HIM GOOD-BYE
Performer	Steam
Album	Steam
Label	Fontana
Writers	Paul Leka, Gary DeCarlo, Dale Frashuer
Producer	Paul Leka

ALL YOU NEED IS LOVE
Performer	The Beatles
Label	Parlophone
Writers	John Lenon, Paul McCartney
Producer	George Martin

EVERYDAY PEOPLE
Performer	Sly and the Family Stone
Album	Stand!
Label	Epic
Writer	Sly Stone
Producer	Sly Stone

RED, RED WINE
Performer	Neil Diamond
Label	Bang
Writer	Neil Diamond
Producers	Jeff Barry, Ellie Greenwich

CRAZY

Performer	Patsy Cline
Label	Decca
Writer	Willie Nelson
Producer	Owen Bradley

DIZZY

Performer	Tommy Roe
Label	ABC Records
Writers	Tommy Roe, Freddy Weller
Producer	Tommy Roe

REUNITED

Performer	Peaches & Herb
Album	2 Hot
Label	MPV/Polydor
Writers	Dino Fekaris, Freddie Perren
Producer	Freddie Perren

AMAZING GRACE

Performer	Judy Collins
Album	Whales and Nightingales
Label	Elektra
Writer	John Newton (1725–1807)
Producer	Mark Abramson

WE'VE ONLY JUST BEGUN

Performer	The Carpenters
Album	Close to You
Label	A&M
Writers	Paul Williams, Roger Nichols
Producer	Jack Daugherty

LIKE TO GET TO KNOW YOU

Performer	Spanky and Our Gang
Album	Like to Get to Know You
Label	Mercury Records
Writer	Stuart Scharf
Producers	Bob Dorough, Stuart Scharf

TRACES

Performer	Classics IV
Album	Greatest Hits
Label	Imperial Records
Writers	Buddy Buie, James Cobb, Emory Gordy
Producer	Buddy Buie

JUST LIKE A WOMAN

Performer	Bob Dylan
Album	Blonde on Blonde
Label	Columbia
Writer	Bob Dylan
Producer	Bob Johnston

WITH A LITTLE HELP FROM MY FRIENDS

Performer	The Beatles
Album	Sgt. Pepper's Lonely Hearts Club Band
Label	Parlophone
Writers	John Lennon, Paul McCartney
Producer	George Martin

I FEEL THE EARTH MOVE

Performer	Carole King
Album	Tapestry
Label	Ode
Writer	Carole King
Producer	Lou Adler

BRIDGE OVER TROUBLED WATER

Performer	Simon & Garfunkel
Album	Bridge Over Troubled Water
Label	Columbia
Writer	Paul Simon
Producers	Roy Halee, Paul Simon, Art Garfunkel

(SITTIN' ON) THE DOCK OF THE BAY

Performer	Otis Redding
Album	The Dock of the Bay
Label	Volt/Atco
Writers	Steve Cropper, Otis Redding
Producer	Steve Cropper

SPINNING WHEEL

Performer	Blood, Sweat & Tears
Album	Blood, Sweat & Tears
Label	Columbia
Writer	David Clayton-Thomas
Producer	James William Guercio

FIRE AND RAIN

Performer	James Taylor
Album	Sweet Baby James
Label	Warner Bros.
Writer	James Taylor
Producer	Peter Asher

MIDNIGHT CONFESSIONS

Performer	Grass Roots
Album	Golden Grass
Label	ABC/Dunhill
Writer	Lou Josie
Producer	Steve Barri

SOUNDS OF SILENCE

Performer	Simon and Garfunkel
Label	Columbia
Writer	Paul Simon
Producer	Tom Wilson

YOU'VE GOT A FRIEND

Performer	James Taylor
Album	Mud Slide Slim and the Blue Horizon
Label	Warner Bros.
Writer	Carole King
Producer	Peter Asher

UNITED WE STAND

Performer	Brotherhood of Man
Label	Deram
Writer	Tony Hiller
Producer	Tony Hiller

DUST IN THE WIND

Performer	Kansas
Label	Kirshner
Writer	Kerry Livgren
Producer	Jeff Glixman

THINK

Performer	Aretha Franklin
Album	Aretha Now
Label	Atlantic
Writers	Aretha Franklin, Teddy White
Producer	Jerry Wexler

THE FIRST TIME EVER I SAW YOUR FACE

Performer	Roberta Flack
Label	Atlantic
Writer	Ewan MacColl
Producer	Joel Dorn

UNDUN

Performer	The Guess Who
Label	Buddha Records
Writer	Randy Bachman
Producer	Jack Richardson

DIARY

Performer	Bread
Album	Best of Bread
Label	Rhino
Writer	David Gates
Producers	David Gates, David McLees

HOTEL CALIFORNIA

Performer	The Eagles
Label	Asylum
Writers	Don Henley, Glenn Frey, Don Felder
Producer	Bill Szymczyk

Also by Fay Campbell

Naked Me: An Assortment of Reflections

Forty-three short
stories, poems, and
lyrics about life,
love and loss

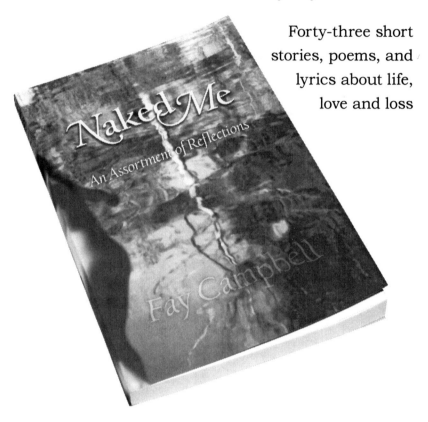

Available at:
  www.FayCampbell.com
  www.Amazon.com
  Book retailers everywhere

For more information about
Hell Outta Dodge, Naked Me, the authors and
their upcoming books, visit the publisher's
web site: **www.BellstoneBooks.com**